LINER

LINER

CHRIS COPPEL

Matador
9 Priory Business Park,
Wistow Road, Kibworth Beauchamp,
Leicestershire. LE8 0RX
Tel: 0116 279 2299
Email: books@troubador.co.uk
Web: www.troubador.co.uk/matador
Twitter: @matadorbooks

ISBN 978 1800462 809

British Library Cataloguing in Publication Data.
A catalogue record for this book is available from the British Library.

Printed and bound in Great Britain by 4edge Limited
Typeset in 11pt Minion Pro by Troubador Publishing Ltd, Leicester, UK

Matador is an imprint of Troubador Publishing Ltd

PROLOGUE

Morgan McCarthy's iPhone alarm began emitting the sound of a croaking frog. He had thought it fun and quirky and picked it from the Apple classic sound library. Hearing it start up again for the third time that morning after putting it on snooze twice was taking all the joy out of it.

At that moment he hated the damn frog.

It was Sunday. A day he should be out having fun with friends or working on his garden or even finishing off installing the new sports exhaust to his vintage Chevy Camaro.

While all valid ways of enjoying the weekend, the reality was that Morgan had few friends, lived in a studio apartment and drove a Prius. He really didn't have much else to do, still, having to go to work on a Sunday just didn't seem right on principle.

He knew that everyone at the National Oceanis and Atmospheric Administration (NOAA) Communications

Center had to work one Sunday a month on a carefully planned roster, but it still bugged the hell out of him.

He pushed the stop icon on his phone, finally shutting up the croaking amphibian, at least for that moment. He considered having a shower but felt that he shouldn't be required to be clean just to sit all day in front of a workstation.

He had a quick look through a plastic milk crate that served as his dirty clothes hamper for a shirt that could pass muster for a second (or third) wearing. He found two possibles, but one had to be disqualified for a hidden barbeque sauce stain on the right sleeve. He settled for the pink Hawaiian with blue dolphins riding massive North Shore surf. It smelled a little funky but a quick squirt of Febreze would take care of that.

He threw on his go-to pair of cargo shorts and his least favourite, food-stained New Balance all terrains. He brushed his teeth without toothpaste as he'd run out two days earlier and had forgotten to get more. He splashed some water on his unshaven face then dabbed it off with a paper towel. The bath towels had been awaiting a wash in the bottom of the milk crate for a couple of weeks. They could work at a pinch, but smelled one stage beyond funky so paper towelling was the obvious solution. He'd planned on doing laundry that weekend but as usual, work got in the way of him getting around to the important things.

He gulped down half a pint of reconstituted orange juice straight from the carton then grabbed a jumbo-sized bean burrito from the freezer. He shoved it in the utility pocket in his cargo shorts then headed down to his car.

The drive to the NOAA Marine Operations and Communication Center in Norfolk only took ten minutes. That was the only good part of working on a Sunday as far as he was concerned. The short drive passed quickly as he sang along to a couple of his favourite Metallica songs at full volume. He didn't even bother to turn the music down when he reached the rolling chain-link security gate. He knew it really pissed off the guys in the gate house but he didn't care.

He grunted to a few co-workers as he made his way through the mainly empty building till he reached his workstation. It was basically just a cubicle but it had been assembled against a wall so that a large LED touchscreen monitor could be mounted directly in front of him.

He dumped himself into his ergonomically engineered desk chair, switched on the monitor, powered up his CPU then logged into NOAA's interactive ocean monitoring interface or NIOMI.

His responsibility was focusing on the North Atlantic Ocean seabed tectonic sensor arrays. The first thing he did every day before he even grabbed coffee was to run a system-wide diagnostic. Everyone told him it was a complete waste of time as the entire system was automated and that any problem with any sensor would show up on the screen, plain as day.

What nobody realised was that while the thirty-minute diagnostic cycle was running, he could take his time getting a hot brew and checking to see if anyone had brought in doughnuts or Danish. If his supervisor asked why he wasn't working, he just had to say that he was running diagnostics.

Nobody had made coffee yet and he certainly wasn't gonna do it. What was worse was that there were no baked goods in sight. He retrieved the burrito from his shorts and tossed it in the microwave.

When he got back to his desk and waited for the diagnostic cycle to finish, he scanned the overnight status logs and saw that there had been some data coming in showing mild earthquakes along the Eurasian and North American subduction plates. That wasn't particularly unusual. What was different was that the sensors were showing movement being recorded for over a hundred miles on one particular undocumented fault line.

That was a large area for a quake that was only reading just above 3.0 on the Richter scale.

The diagnostics showed no anomalies with any sensors or the support network. As he reached over to grab what was left of his microwaved burrito, the centre of his monitor screen blossomed with red flashing circles as sensors began reporting seismological readings in excess of 6.5.

He watched as the numbers increased along the fault. The quake peaked at 8.1. The epicentre appeared to be directly under sensor number forty-seven which was anchored to the ocean floor almost five miles below the surface.

It took nearly half an hour before most of the sensors stopped flashing and turned from red back to their operational standby colour of green.

The exception was number forty-seven. It continued flashing red despite the seismic readings dropping to zero.

Morgan ran a new diagnostic sequence through the sensor's onboard CPU but got no return readings.

Suddenly number forty-seven's red circle began flashing diagonal black bars.

Morgan took a bite of his burrito while he debated calling Operations Control to report a bad sensor. It wasn't a cheap call to make. A research ship would have to be dispatched to the area then they would have to send down a submersible. If they couldn't fix it on the bottom, it would have to be brought to the surface. When you're talking about repairs or recovery five miles down, – it was an expensive operation which meant filling out reams of justification forms.

He didn't want to make the call until he was sure the unit wouldn't reboot itself. Obviously, it had had a pretty good shake up, but they usually came back on line given enough time to calm down.

He wouldn't have been so reluctant to make the call had it not been for the fact that he'd called in a deep-water sensor fault six months earlier. In that instance, the sensor had gone completely dark. There was no info going to, or coming from it. A ship had been diverted and a submersible lowered.

They found no trace of the unit on the ocean floor. It wasn't until months later when it reappeared over fifty miles south of its previous position that they were eventually able to work out the problem. A fibre-optic support ship had raised a cable for repair and somehow snagged the sensor and brought it to the surface. It was found that some idiot on board had thought he'd get in trouble so he somehow worked out how to switch the unit off. He then waited three months until he felt he was in the clear then turned it back on and tossed it back into the ocean.

What the guy didn't know was that he had only turned off the transmit system. The unit had continued monitoring everything the entire time. The moment he turned the sensor back on and tossed it into the water, it didn't just transmit its new location, it ran full diagnostics on itself. The data it spewed out showed exactly where it had been for the entire three months.

It wasn't hard to match the sensor's GPS location log with that of a particular cable-repair ship.

Despite Morgan having carried out his responsibilities to the letter, he became the brunt of jokes concerning anything that went missing within the NOAA sphere.

He had no intention of letting that happen again.

He tried sending another diagnostic ping to the unit but nothing happened. He repeated the process for the next two hours. The unit was definitely transmitting and was still in its designated location. It just wasn't communicating.

He had to believe that this one was legit. He just prayed that it wouldn't turn into something else.

He took a deep breath then reached for the phone.

CHAPTER
ONE

David couldn't keep his eyes off the beautiful young woman across the table from him. She seemed to almost glow under the dimmed chandeliers in the first-class dining room. She was deeply involved in a conversation with a middle-aged couple seated to her left.

She seemed completely oblivious to David even though they had sat at the same table for days sharing every meal together.

He knew just by looking at her that he wasn't her type. Sadly, that didn't stop his growing infatuation which he knew would be unrequited and thus become yet another stress in his already overburdened life.

A loud but melodic three-note chime interrupted the lunch service.

"Ladies and gentlemen. This is your captain speaking. I apologise for interrupting your lunch, however we have been

advised of an unusual phenomenon that has occurred some distance from our location. A vessel has notified us that a rogue wave has formed over eighty miles from our current position and could potentially pass within viewing distance of the Oceanis. Please know that this ship can withstand any wave the sea might offer up, however, if we feel that the wave could intersect with our course, we will sound the alarm in order for everyone to brace themselves. In the meantime, the wave should become visible on the horizon in a matter of minutes and in my opinion would be worth seeing. I must again stress that this vessel and all those aboard are in no danger. The SS Oceanis was built to specifications way beyond what would be required to manage a wave of any size. I suggest that those who can, should go on deck and enjoy this natural wonder."

The chimes sounded again, signifying the end of the communication.

A ripple of nervous yet excited laughter rolled through the massive dining room. People calmly left their lunches and headed topside.

David looked across the table to check if the young woman was going to leave the table. He saw that she already had. She was flanked on either side by her father and mother.

The wave was expected to be extraordinary.

Almost every passenger had found a vantage point on the starboard side. The captain made a second announcement with a revised heading for the rare wave and advised that it was possible that it could intersect with the *Oceanis*. He again stressed that no one was in any danger but advised everyone to shelter and brace should they be told to do so.

Folk being folks – they did the exact opposite.

They jammed every spare inch of deck space, just in the hopes of seeing what the captain described as a once-in-a-lifetime phenomenon.

At first it was impossible to see. It was, after all, over forty miles away – the maximum distance the ship's radar could detect. Then, right at the horizon line, they could see an irregularity of the earth's curvature.

They watched in rapt excitement as the wave grew in size. It seemed to be moving slowly, but that was an illusion. The tsunami brought on by the slippage of adjoining tectonic plates was moving at close to 400 miles per hour.

Passengers marvelled at the majesty of the thing. It reached from one end of the horizon to the other. The ship sounded its horn with seven short blasts and one long.

The crowd applauded. They loved that the captain was getting excited as well. They may have felt differently had they known that the seven short and one long horn blasts were only used in the event of a shipboard emergency.

A new sound reached the passengers as emergency klaxons began to reverberate throughout the ship. A voice began repeating almost robotically – 'Shelter and brace' – 'Shelter and brace'.

There was a third sound that slowly became audible. It was from the wave itself. It was a low-frequency rumble that soon dominated all other sound.

The passengers suddenly felt the ship drop as the water beneath them was sucked away from under the keel to feed the rising tsunami.

The feeling of celebration ebbed from the crowd. The wave was no longer a distant attraction. At less than ten miles from the massive liner, they could start to register its height.

Even at that distance, they realised two things. It was bigger than anyone could have thought possible and it was going to reach the ship.

The captain was trying to move the mighty liner into a position where it would meet the wave at a forty-five-degree approach angle. That was the SOP for addressing high-wave contact. The last thing they wanted to do was have it hit them abeam. Despite being one of the largest liners afloat, a wave that size would flip it within seconds.

The wave continued its approach. The closer it got, the faster the approach appeared. The liner was over 150 feet tall from the waterline, yet the wave was already towering above it.

The force of the water being sucked into the monster to feed its increased thirst was causing the ship to heel to starboard even as it tried to straighten so as to face it.

The passengers were no longer joyous onlookers. Panic had set in. People began screaming and running. They were on a ship – albeit a huge one, but still a ship. There was nowhere to run to. The wave was now of such a height that it began blocking light. Its shadow cloaked the entire vessel. On the bridge, the crew knew the horrific truth.

No one was going to survive. The rake of the wave was such that they had no chance of climbing over it. They were not going to be able to crest the wave wall and would almost certainly be torn asunder.

David Easton was one of the few passengers to stay at the railings on the Sun Deck and wait out the inevitable. He wasn't brave or foolhardy. He just wanted to see what was going to kill him.

The liner started to tilt upwards as the bow reached the very base of the wave. It started to climb the steep wall of water but despite the ship's mighty engines, it began to slide, stern first, back down the wave wall.

There was nothing beyond the wall except more water. It wasn't really a wave. It was a giant swell created when the earth's crust fractured and thrust upwards.

The sleek, black-hulled ocean liner buried its stern into the base of the wave and was immediately sucked back into the growing mass of water. It began to tip backwards pivoting on its stern. The bow then plunged beneath the surface ploughing a path to the bottom of the ocean.

David had held on to the rail with every ounce of his being, but was sucked away the moment the liner submerged. At first, he was conscious of the water ripping the air from his body. He even felt the force of the water as he was dragged and pushed in a million directions at once.

Then he felt nothing at all.

CHAPTER
TWO

David Easton awoke screaming. He was drenched in sweat and couldn't seem to breathe. His hands held on to the bed head as if his life depended on it. He still tasted the salt water he'd ingested – or at least dreamt he'd ingested.

He turned on the bedside light and cautiously looked around his first-class cabin. The meticulously varnished walls and matching wood furniture gleamed back at him. The cabin's two curtained portholes with a built-in chest of drawers below looked to David, in his frame of mind, like the squared-off face of a boxer. Especially as he'd left a lower drawer open with a single sock draped over the side making it look like a tongue.

He'd been having the same dream every night since being at sea. It seemed as if he'd been having it for weeks yet he knew the entire crossing was only six days. It wasn't a pleasant experience. He wasn't that enamoured with the ocean to start with. To feel it fill his lungs and rip his body apart on a nightly basis just wasn't fair. Especially when one considered how much he'd paid for the first-class transatlantic crossing.

David used to love being on the water when he was younger. He would spend all day on boats or rafts or just about anything that floated. Just after his sixteenth birthday, a friend had convinced him that what he really needed to try was kayaking. He was game to give it a go.

They drove up to the Finger Lakes in upstate New York on a warm, late spring day. They rented a couple of kayaks and his friend gave him some basic instruction.

David had been a little concerned about being so tightly wedged into the tiny craft but got the hang of it quickly. They had been on the water for over an hour when a powerboat tore past them at full speed. Its wake hit David's kayak on its left side. The craft instantly rolled upside down.

David had been shown how to exit an overturned boat and had practised the manoeuvre a number of times. The problem was that he'd practised without any cargo on board. Out of sight of the boat rental office, David had wedged a windbreaker and a picnic basket between his legs within the front compartment of the kayak.

Once he was upside down, he realised that he couldn't get free of the fiberglass vessel. His legs were stuck in a spread position because of the basket. No matter what he tried, he couldn't free them. He started to panic. He tried to right the kayak but the weight of the filled cooler was acting like ballast. Nothing he did seemed to help. Within moments, he'd swallowed his first mouthful of lake water and started to cough while upside down and submerged.

He suddenly knew that he was going to die. He stopped struggling and let the cold water enter his lungs.

Three other boats including his friend's, reached him and righted the kayak. David was unconscious and looked dead. On one of the responding boats was a lifeguard. The young man forcefully dragged him out of the kayak and laid him facing upwards on the slatted wooden decking of his inflatable craft. He began to perform CPR immediately.

It took over ninety seconds before David regurgitated his first lungful of water.

By the time they reached the wooden dock, an ambulance was there waiting. He had to spend the night in the hospital for observation but was released the following morning. The attending doctor told him that he was very lucky to be alive. They estimated that he had stopped breathing for over two minutes.

David recovered fully with no further health repercussions. His emotional condition, however, had been irrevocably changed. From that moment on, he never ventured onto open water again.

That was until he suddenly came to the questionable realisation that a transatlantic voyage was the solution to all his problems.

David wasn't a rich man. He'd held a good paying position as a micro-biologist, but that was before the divorce and custody battle. He'd come out of those a far poorer individual – both financially and psychologically.

The fact that his ex-wife's father had been the managing director of the company where he'd worked, suddenly became a major problem. The old man had patiently waited until the divorce was granted, then fired him on the spot.

David had spent his thirty-eighth birthday alone in a studio rental apartment on the wrong side of Fifth Avenue, in New York. The year only become more sordid, as he learned that his ex-father-in-law had blackballed him from every club, restaurant and also apparently, from every possible job in the entire city.

Considering that the custody battle had deprived him of almost all access to his children – he was not in a good place. 1962 had become a very bad year.

After having spent an exceptionally bleak day wallowing in self-pity, David decided that he wasn't going to take it any more. Not in a brave 'face the obstacle' sort of way. No. After much contemplation and cheap bourbon, David had decided to end his life.

Being a thorough and detail-orientated man who had no qualms about deep research, he'd spent two entire days at the New York Central Library reading up on the best methods of suicide. He'd found it quite astonishing just how many books on the subject actually existed. There were thin pamphlets, thick dusty tomes and even ones with terrifyingly graphic illustrations.

After all the investigating, he was even more confused about the best possible process for a clean and pain-free suicide.

While walking by the Hudson River one exceptionally blustery morning, he admired the row of majestic ocean liners being provisioned for their next voyage. He'd always wanted to travel on one, but because of his deep-rooted fear of water, he'd had to satisfy himself by observing the luxury flotilla from the shore.

Then it had come to him. What a gloriously eccentric thing it would be, to end one's life by diving off of the stern of such a vessel in the middle of some vast body of water.

David then made the ultimate decision that he would find the most glamorous transatlantic crossing available and treat himself to a first-class ticket. He planned to make the most of the first four days of the voyage, then have one final lavish dinner, after which he would dive graciously into the great briny and allow himself to sink down into a trouble-free oblivion.

It had cost him almost 500 dollars for the passage and another hundred just to have the appropriate clothing for the voyage. At least for the period he would still be on board.

David spent the next few months quietly severing himself from the city and his life. He had few friends and even those turned out to be fair-weather.

He tried to obtain permission from his wife to see his children for the last time, though that last part was obviously omitted.

She refused.

Bolstered literally by a life-ending schedule, David walked into their school unannounced, and sought each one out in their respective classrooms. He lovingly bade them each farewell and was not surprised when neither seemed to care. His ex-wife had somehow managed to poison them against him. He walked out of the exorbitantly expensive private school feeling even more despondent than when he'd gone in.

The school threatened legal action against his uninvited intrusion. His ex-wife threatened even more legal action, but David didn't care anymore.

He wasn't going to be around.

If the weather and the engines of the *SS Oceanis* obliged, he would be nothing more than food for the deepest sea feeders by the time any of their threats could be enacted.

On 12 May David boarded what was considered to be the world's most luxurious ocean liner, with the intention of enjoying every second of the transatlantic crossing right up until the moment of his death.

CHAPTER
THREE

David found the concept of time on a ship at sea to be strangely elastic and interminable, while at the same time appearing somehow ephemeral.

He couldn't quite remember the details of the actual boarding, yet he knew for a fact that he obviously had to have boarded. He wasn't alone in feeling a bit discombobulated. Apparently, it was a normal sensation. He'd discussed the subject with other passengers and they all told him they felt the same way, but reminded him that that was the whole point of an ocean crossing. The sensory deprivation from the cacophony of the real-world din is one of the most cherished parts of the entire experience.

David checked the bedside clock and saw that it was only 5 a.m. He swung his legs out of the bed and snuggled his feet into his newly purchased, sheepskin-lined, tartan slippers.

He checked by the cabin door and was delighted to see that the daily onboard newspaper, amusingly called *The Daily Log*, had been slid silently under his door.

There was never any news as such, but it gave a report of the weather, sea conditions and the general events aboard ship for that day.

The weather looked to be foggy again, though quite mild; the sea would have only a minor swell which would hardly be felt by passengers.

There was to be a shuffleboard competition on Lido Deck, clay-pigeon shooting on the fantail and a costume party in the Grand Salon starting at 19:00 hours. He had no intention of competing in a game of shuffleboard. He had watched it the other day and realised that the competitors all seemed to be octogenarian, or at least looked the part.

He would definitely try the shooting, especially as the shotgun had been one of the more recommended methods of self-termination according to his research.

How delightfully ironic to be taught how to use his second favourite method of suicide while standing on the deck of his preferred one.

The one activity listed in the *Log* that he was most excited about was the costume party. David had never fared well at parties. He had trouble mingling and became tongue-tied and socially clumsy. The only exception had been at a costume party many years earlier when he had found that by simply covering his own face, his insecurities vanished. He had been able for the first time to actually enjoy a social gathering. He hoped the shipboard party would have the same effect.

He smiled to himself as he slipped on a pair of rubber-soled boat shoes, a pair of Bermuda shorts and a grey singlet. Being so early in the day, he would doubtless have Promenade Deck all to himself and be able to have a brisk walk behind the protective glass that sheltered the deck from the open air.

His cabin was only one deck below so he decided to take the stairs up the one flight. As he stepped out of the watertight hatchway door, he smelled the wonderful combination of teak and fresh air infused with ocean salt. He also saw the dense fog that had accompanied the ship for days. He couldn't even see far enough down the hull to view where it met the Atlantic, twelve decks below.

David did a couple of toe touches and knee bends to warm up, then began a vigorous stroll. The designers of the *Oceanis* had been very clever and had devised a way for Promenade Deck to be unobstructed forward and aft, allowing passengers to walk the entire circuit without having to stop at each end of the vessel, open a door, transition a hallway, then exit another door to re-join the promenade area.

The *Oceanis* had been the first ocean liner in the world to have the new unrestricted layout. The designer had been influenced by the growing craze of people who chose to run for pleasure. David would never understand that concept, but if it meant that he could walk in a circle the entire way around the ship, he wished the runners well.

He completed three laps of the deck and decided to call it a day. He didn't want to be seen sweating in a public place. He descended the stairway back to Main Deck and his cabin.

He ran himself a bath while listening to one of the onboard radio stations. He found one that was playing some relatively current music. He wasn't hip enough to like all of the new music, but some of it was quite catchy.

'Sugar Shack' was just ending. It was followed by the new group from England called The Beatles. The song was 'I Saw Her Standing There'. He quite liked it, though the oohing he found to be a tad odd. He'd recently seen a picture of the group and wondered why they would intentionally limit their audience appeal with those ridiculous haircuts.

Bathed and talcum-powdered, he dressed in a pair of beige slacks and a navy blue, short-sleeved shirt. He gave himself a quick glance in the dressing mirror, felt the usual disappointment at not having been born dashingly handsome, then made his way to C Deck and the first-class dining salon.

There were already quite a few people in the restaurant lobby waiting for the velvet rope to be removed at 7 a.m. sharp. A few of his fellow passengers looked a little worse for wear. Others looked sprightly and were chomping at the bit to get the day started so they could take part in as many onboard amenities as possible.

The rope was discreetly removed at the appointed time and David headed to his assigned table. He'd been very lucky that he wasn't the only single person at table seven. Diana Olson was the second, and was seated directly across from him with her mother on one side and her father on the other.

Diana was attractive in an outdoorsy way. Her chestnut shoulder-length hair always seemed to shine, whatever the lighting. She had a cute, upturned nose that was enhanced by a sprinkling of freckles on her cheeks. Her blue eyes were a shade of aquamarine that seemed to change in hue according to her mood. Despite her good looks and infectious laugh, Diana was far from perfect. The poor girl suffered from one highly disabling affliction.

That affliction was her mother, Myra Olson.

Her parents had clearly brought their daughter on the voyage in the hopes of finding her a suitable husband, yet her mother kept her so closely guarded that even the most confident suiter would think twice about having to deal with her constant chaperone.

At twenty-nine, Diana was considered almost past marrying age. David had at first assumed that she would be as desperate as her mother to find her a mate before the starting gates firmly closed once she turned thirty.

As it happened, she couldn't have cared less. She worked as an assistant editor for a new lady's fashion magazine in New York. She was perfectly happy not being saddled with a husband who, one assumed, would almost certainly not permit her to work – especially not for some fashion rag.

Diana turned out to have a lovely sense of humour and took her mother's efforts to find her a mate with a grain of salt. She and David had struck up a comfortable friendship, based mainly on their mutually jaded and sarcastic view of the other passengers.

On the first night at sea they all met for the first time at their assigned table, number seven. Diana's mother had spotted David as a potential threat and had been concerned that he was going to get in the way of her plans to introduce Diana to the right sort of men. David found it odd that he was considered a threat yet was apparently not suitable to be on the eligibility list. He couldn't quite decide if he was offended or relieved.

Of course, he knew that he couldn't be in the running anyway – not with his imminent suicide on the cards, but Diana's mother didn't know that. He therefore became obsessively curious about which of his traits had eliminated him from any consideration seemingly before he had even opened his mouth.

David had been in a highly respectable job, earning more than a decent living. He knew he wasn't Cary Grant, but surely looks were secondary when trying to dispose of your unwed daughter.

He realised early on that those obsessive concerns had to stop. He had to keep reminding himself that he wasn't even going to be around in a few days and therefore needed to try and get some enjoyment out of those that were left.

The other three couples at table seven were charming. Wendy and Ron Stanford were from Utah and had made their money through beekeeping and introducing organic honey to the entire state. They were in their sixties, seemed to love life and were natural-born storytellers. Especially Ron, who seemed to have lived a dozen different lives before finding and marrying Wendy.

The Anderson's – Alan and Sofie – were born and bred New Yorkers. They owned TV stations all the way up the east coast as far as Maine. Both now in their seventies, they had nothing but money and some time left in which to spend it. Sofie was quiet and for the most part let Alan do the talking. Alan took full advantage.

His family had originated in the Bronx and Alan had some amazing stories of his battles to get educated and then ultimately, rich.

The third couple, Julie and Tom Krabb, were from California and had turned a small fruit stand in Oxnard into one of the state's biggest supermarket chains. Krabb Premier Markets were in every town on the west coast. They were heading to England to have meetings about opening a branch in London.

They were serious people with few stories and little patience for small talk – at least until Julie had had her second glass of wine, at which point her neutral California accent developed a distinct southern twang. She had stories about her early life in Georgia that could set your ears alight.

All in all, David felt he had landed on a good table. He wasn't a great fan of communal dining, but for breakfast, that was your only choice other than room service unless you were in one of the premier suites. They had the privilege of having breakfast in the Veranda Grill. David had tried the exclusive grill once for dinner, but being seated alone was a little dire and conversation when sitting by yourself could be highly stilted.

After a breakfast of scrambled eggs, crispy bacon, rye toast and superb coffee, David went on his daily exploratory trek around the vast ship.

The *Oceanis* was 980 feet long, weighed just over 80,000 tons and could carry up to 2,100 passengers in two classes. In addition, there was a crew of just over a thousand to ensure that passengers were spoiled, pampered and kept safe.

When she went into service in 1957, she was considered to be the most luxurious ocean liner ever built. She was also the fastest. She had won the highly sought-after Blue Riband award in 1957 and 1959 for the fastest Atlantic crossing.

The ship had a shopping arcade, a 700-seat cinema, a live performance venue, a well-stocked library, a casino, two outdoor swimming pools, squash courts, a beauty parlour, a barbershop, a dentist, an infirmary, a Turkish bath, a steam room as well as a number of restaurants and bars.

There was no excuse for not being able to find a pleasing activity at any time of the day.

David enjoyed prowling around on his own. He didn't like to use the wall charts or the maps that showed where you were and how to get to where you wanted to be. He preferred to find his own way around the ship through trial and error.

The crew wasn't mad about passengers snooping below decks, but became far more forgiving upon finding out that one was from first class. David was amazed at the difference in treatment one received just for paying more.

He had already explored most of the decks at the stern of the ship and decided to seek out the main engine room for that day's quest. He knew it had to be located just aft of the second funnel so, by imagining its journey down into the boiler room, he could guess from which point to start the search.

He began from the dining room where he'd just eaten. It was on a low deck anyway so it made sense. He walked aft of the giant room and found a staircase with no signs denoting its path. That gave him hope.

He walked down a utilitarian stairway, and came to a closed door that was clearly labelled for crew use only. He ignored the notice and walked through the watertight doorway. Beyond it, any semblance of luxury ended. Gone was the elegant carpeting and finely inlaid wood-panelled walls.

He was in an area designed for work, not for pampering and relaxation. He walked along the linoleum floor, careful not to hit his head on low-hanging piping that ran the length of the passageway.

His footsteps echoed against the steel walls. He saw no sign of any access to the engine room but did find himself at the entry to the ship's infirmary. At least he assumed that to be the case. The big red cross on the wall next to the open door was the clue.

He poked his nose in to see if it was safe to have a quick peek. There didn't seem to be anyone around. The place was surprisingly small for a huge boat. It had a bright white corridor with three rooms on either side and a double door at the far end.

The place smelled of rubbing alcohol, menthol and something else. Something just slightly sour.

David heard voices at the far end of the corridor and decided that as he had made it that far, he may as well have a gander. His first-class status would resolve any ruffled feathers should someone take issue with his presence.

As he approached the double doors, they swung open and a deck officer in full dress whites strode out. He passed David at speed.

"You shouldn't be down here," he advised before exiting the infirmary. David could hear the officer run off down the passageway. He turned and looked through the open doors. Three people were staring down at someone lying on a stainless-steel examination table. The man looked to be a crew member judging from his dark steward's suit. His starched white shirt was open to the waist.

It was the area above the belt line that seemed to fascinate the three onlookers. There was a dark green mass that covered him from just below his navel to the base of his sternum.

David had never seen anything like it before. The discoloration was slightly translucent showing something black beneath it. The onlookers must have sensed David's presence, as they all turned towards him at the same time. Even the patient on the table turned to face him.

David recognised the ship's doctor, William Aikens, from the first night's welcome-aboard party. The other two he didn't know. The man being examined however, David knew very well. He was the ship's steward assigned to David's cabin and the rest of that section of Main Deck.

He smiled at David. "Sorry about this, Mr Easton. Is there something you need for your cabin?"

"Are you all right, Andrew?" David asked.

"Nothing to worry about, sir. Just some blasted rash. The doc here doesn't think it's contagious. A bit of ointment and an aspirin and I'll be right as rain."

The doctor looked at David and nodded his head in agreement with the steward's prognosis.

"I'm afraid you'll need to leave us to get on with the evaluation," the doctor said politely yet with a stern undertone.

"Of course," David replied. He suddenly felt embarrassed at having intruded.

He gave Andrew a positive smile then left the infirmary to find his way back to the passenger decks. Any thought of continuing his search for the elusive engine room that day was gone completely. He felt he had caused enough disruption for one morning.

He hoped he would see Andrew back on duty later in the day so he could apologise. He couldn't help wondering what exactly could cause a rash of that nature.

David didn't get to see his steward back on duty later that day. By mid-afternoon, Andrew had vanished. No one seemed to know where he'd gone. The doctor had signed him out of the infirmary shortly after David's unwelcome visit. He had clocked in for his return to duty. Had served tea in three cabins, lunch in seven cabins, then had simply disappeared.

Andrew became known to the senior officers on board as patient number one. He was the first known person infected with what they coined as, 'the green plague'.

CHAPTER
FOUR

David returned to his cabin feeling mildly out of sorts. Seeing his steward in that condition had left him with a sense of being untethered from reality. For the first time since boarding the *Oceanis*, he felt undeserving of the lavish surroundings and pampered treatment.

He was living a lie and was doing so in front of everyone. That wasn't who he was. At least not the person he was before the divorce. The entire trip was a charade masking what was to be his final act of complete cowardice. It wasn't that he was doubting his original intentions. It was just that as each day passed, the whole premise became almost too maudlin to consider. He still wanted to die, but at the same time realised that dragging it out was pointless, and if he were to be honest with himself, somewhat selfish as well.

Each day, he touched the lives of people he hadn't met before. It wasn't that these encounters were that meaningful to anyone, but when the time came for him to make the big leap, more and more people would have become aware of his existence and therefore would feel some emotion, no matter how fleeting, at his demise.

David realised that he was becoming depressingly self-absorbed. He decided at that moment that he would cease dragging out the inevitable and carry out the planned high dive right after the costume party that night.

As soon as he'd made the decision he felt as if an enormous weight had been lifted from his shoulders. Just the knowledge that his loneliness and emotional exhaustion would be over in a matter of hours actually raised his spirits.

He no longer felt like sulking in his cabin; rather, he wanted to do something interesting. Something fun. He remembered the clay-pigeon shooting scheduled for that morning. He checked his watch and realised that it was due to start in just a few minutes. He gave his face a quick wash then turned on the cold water to brush his teeth.

Once he had completed the recommended number of brush strokes per tooth, he filled a glass with water to rinse away the foamy residue.

He almost gagged. The water tasted of salt. Lots of it. He tried the bath tap but that too was salty.

With no alternative he swished the saline solution around his mouth then quickly spat it out.

He made a mental note to let his steward know about the water issue. Having no experience of ocean voyaging, he realised that such an occurrence could be completely normal. David, however, had a basic knowledge of the principles of plumbing and couldn't imagine how the fresh water supply could become tainted with what he had to assume was sea water.

He made his way to Sun Deck then walked as far aft as he could go. It wasn't hard to find the shooting station. All he had to do was follow the sound. The fog seemed to trap the percussive noise of the gunfire causing it to reverberate across the entire exterior of the ship.

David watched for a few minutes and saw that the regular dynamics of the sport had had to change because of the fog. Where normally a shooter would have a couple of seconds to hit the launched clay disc, there was now only a millisecond before the target vanished into the grey mist and disappeared from sight.

No one was hitting the clay pigeons. They just flew off the spring-loaded launcher and before the shooter could get a good sighting they seemed to magically disappear, such was the thickness of the fog.

It finally came to his turn. He felt he'd come up with a solution of sorts. Instead of trying to lead the gun ahead of the projectile, as was the norm, David positioned his sights on the trajectory he'd observed from the previous shooters.

He shouted pull, then fired immediately. The clay pigeon exploded less than ten feet from the launcher.

In a show of pure bravado, he handed the shotgun back to the deck steward and announced that he couldn't top that, so he may as well stop there.

His fellow shooters looked on with envy.

The fact was, the recoil from the gun had hurt so badly, his right shoulder was completely numb. He couldn't have fired the damn gun again if his life depended on it.

He headed for the Neptune Cocktail Lounge to have a quick drink before lunch. It was one of his favourite places on the ship. Not just because of the alcohol but rather because of its incredible view. It was the only public space on the *Oceanis* that faced forward.

Sipping a Tom Collins while looking down on the foredeck of one of the greatest ocean liners in the world was not something granted to most mortal men. David knew it, and tried to find any excuse to sit at their floor-to-ceiling windows as often as possible.

Revitalised by the cocktail and with his shoulder having regained some feeling, he made his way below deck to the dining room.

He was surprised to find that only the Stanfords had chosen to eat lunch there on that day.

Just as he was tucking into his shrimp cocktail starter, he saw Diana and her parents enter the room. He felt his pulse quicken. He was just about to stand and greet the Olsons when Myra spotted him at the table. Without any attempt at subtlety, she grabbed her daughter and husband in each hand and steered them right out of the dining room and through the lobby.

Ron Stanford couldn't help but laugh.

"I doubt you've noticed yet, young David, but that mamma hen has no intention in this lifetime of letting you near her young chick!"

David couldn't help but laugh and ended up having a very enjoyable lunch with the Stanfords, despite his earlier rebuff. During a lull in the conversation, David asked if they had been having any trouble with the water in their cabin's bathroom.

"I'm not sure I know what you mean by trouble?" Wendy replied.

"Anything odd? Mine has gone salty," David said.

"Can't think of anything," Ron added. "Except we did find a piece of seaweed in the toilet yesterday. Does that count?"

After lunch, David had only one mission. It had dawned on him that if he was to attend the costume party, he would most certainly need a costume. There had been mention in the *Daily Log* that one of the shops in the arcade would have a selection for passengers to choose from.

He found the formal wear and costume shop among the other pricy establishments within the shopping arcade. He was stunned to learn that almost every costume had been reserved within moments of sailing. Apparently, only a cruising novice would wait until the day of the actual party.

All that was left for a man was a Zorro costume. David was actually delighted at the sole option. The dashing cape and the mysterious black mask actually appealed to him. Being neither dashing nor mysterious in real life, adopting the swashbuckling arrogance of Zorro was the perfect alter ego for one night.

He returned to his cabin and immediately tried on the ensemble. He liked the look. The only slight problem was that the sword was made of plastic and at some point had developed a curve halfway along the blade. He was determined to find a way of straightening it before the party.

David had time to kill before the big event and still had a nagging urge to find out what had happened to his steward despite his earlier feeling of embarrassment. He retraced his steps from the morning and managed to find the infirmary again.

This time he waited in the passageway and knocked on the door. There was no response. He eased the door open and saw that the place looked empty. He was about to give up when he heard the sound of a chair scraping on the floor. It came from one of the rooms off the infirmary hallway.

David approached the door and listened. The door suddenly flew open. Dr Williams poked his head out of the room making sure he kept the door pressed against him so that David couldn't see inside.

"What in heaven's name do you think you are doing?" he barked. "You have no business here."

"And you have no right to talk to me with that tone of voice. I came down here out of concern for Andrew, my steward. Nobody seems to have seen him."

"I apologise for the tone, but I am with a patient and don't like to be disturbed. As for Andrew, I sent him back to work soon after you saw him. Where he is now is none of my business. I suggest you relax and enjoy the voyage."

Williams gave him a forced smile then retracted his head back into what David assumed was an examination room. He stood there for a moment wondering whether to push for more information as it was obvious that the doctor was lying but couldn't imagine why.

He decided to give it twenty-four hours. If there was still no sign of Andrew, he would have a word with the purser.

The costume party was held in the first-class Grand Salon. A jazz quartet was tucked into an unobtrusive corner and was playing some very danceable up-tempo tunes. The moment David walked into the three-storey tall lounge, he realised that a great many of the passengers took costume parties very seriously. At least half the crowd must have brought their own costumes on board with them. The scene looked like something from the court of Louis XIV. He had never seen so many vintage ball gowns and exquisitely crafted masks. Some were bejewelled with sequins and rhinestones.

Then there were the passengers like him that had relied on the rental shop to have something fun and original. David could see three gorillas, two werewolves and eight Draculas and that was without really looking.

There were also a good number of guests dressed as famous movie stars. There were a few Marilyn Monroes, a couple of Carmen Mirandas (replete with fruit salad head gear), a Lucille Ball and for the men – a good spattering of Clark Gables, James Cagneys and even a few John Waynes.

David felt he'd found the perfect compromise with his costume. It was somewhere between audaciously glamorous and mundanely unimaginative.

David glanced occasionally down at his sword to make sure it had remained straight. He had asked his new room steward to run a hot iron over it and though the man had been highly dubious of the outcome, it appeared to have done the trick.

David was still not enamoured with the obligatory small talk, but was, however, perfectly happy to wander aimlessly around the sumptuous lounge checking out all the costumes. If approached, he struck a sword-fighting pose and asked, in a bad Spanish accent, "Do you dare to question the great Zorro?"

After a couple of hours, he decided that he'd done his bit. He'd circled the vast salon more than a dozen times and even had a few conversations with totally anonymous strangers.

As he turned to leave, Errol Flynn appeared to step in front of him blocking his exit. The resemblance was uncanny. The pirate costume was almost too authentic. The faux Errol drew his sword and prodded David in the chest. David was shocked to feel that, unlike his own droopy plastic replica, Errol's sword seemed to be the real thing.

"You're not thinking of abandoning ship so soon, are you?"

The impression was spot on though the voice was just a smidge too high. David studied the face more closely while Errol just stood there smiling.

"Diana?"

"How dare you refer to me by that name, oh masked avenger!"

She prodded him with her sword again.

"Ouch! That thing's really sharp, you know!"

"Perhaps a duel is in order?" Diana replied, still in character.

"I don't think it would be a fair battle, I'm afraid."

David waved his cheap plastic sword back and forth a few times. Something in the ironing process had made the plastic even more bendy. It now drooped at ninety degrees when flexed.

"That is truly a pathetic weapon, good sir. If that's the best you can offer, perhaps I should venture further afoot to seek a more noble challenger," Diana said.

"Are we still talking about swords?" David replied.

"You really don't get out much, do you?" she teased as she dropped the pirate impression. "Let's get you a drink and some air."

She grabbed his hand and whisked him past the other inebriated partygoers. She led him up the grand staircase to Promenade Deck then up an exterior stairway aft to Sun Deck.

The Atlantic View bar was tucked away next to the first-class library and smoking room. David, who considered himself to be the great explorer, hadn't even known it existed. The bar was small but invitingly elegant. The mahogany walls gave way to dark green leather armchairs and what looked to be antique side tables. The bar itself had a black granite top that was so highly polished, one felt one could actually reach into it.

"Good evening, Alex," Diana greeted the bartender.

Alex seemed sincerely pleased to see her.

"Alex has been the bartender on the *Oceanis* since its first voyage," Diana advised. "Alex, this dashing swordsman is David. We met having both been trapped at the same dining table."

"It's a pleasure meeting you, David." Alex must have been in his sixties but still had a mischievous twinkle in his eyes. "I see you have both partaken of our masked ball."

David turned to Diana with a straight face. "No, we haven't. In fact, I didn't know there was one. Did you, dear?"

Alex smiled warmly at the joke. "I believe I know Miss Olson's pleasure. With what may I tempt you, sir?"

"I'm open for an adventure. I'll have what she's having."

Alex turned his back on the pair as he started preparing the surprise cocktail.

"So, where's your security detail tonight?" David asked.

"I convinced my mother that being dressed as a man plus being heavily armed would doubtless put off most men who were hunting for easy prey."

Alex gently placed their drinks before them. He was grinning.

David looked down in amazement.

"Boilermakers! You sneak up to probably the most exclusive bar on the Atlantic Ocean and drink boilermakers?"

"What's wrong with that? Do you find it strange because I'm a woman?"

"I think it's strange because you're not a stevedore," he replied.

Alex chuckled to himself.

Diana tried not to smile. She had spent a great deal of her life ensuring that she did not follow the traditional mould of a submissive young woman of the sixties. She had been ready to scrap with David if he'd shown any disdain for her drinking a man's drink. His answer had surprised and amused her. There seemed to be more to her table mate than she had originally thought. Then again, this was the first time the two had spoken without the entire table as their audience.

"So, shot or depth charge?" Diana asked.

"I'm not a complete animal," David replied as he picked up the shot glass of whisky and held it out as a toast. Diana clinked hers against his before they both downed the amber liquid in one. David shuddered then took a long drink from the pint of lager in front of him. Diana did the same.

Two boilermakers later, David turned to her with a serious though slightly glazed expression.

"I have to ask," David slurred slightly. "You are obviously an independent woman. You have a good career. You have some charm, and in the right light are really quite attractive."

"Are you getting to a question there, Zorro?"

"So, why do you let your mother run your life for you? It doesn't seem to fit," David said.

"She doesn't run my life at all."

"It sure looks that way," David added.

"May I finish?" She gave him a fake glare. "First of all, I don't live with my parents. I have a tiny walk-up in the village. I only see them probably once every two months."

"But this trip…"

"Will you please shut up and let me finish?" She shook her head. "Nine months ago, my mother was diagnosed with cancer. We really thought we were going to lose her. She underwent some truly awful chemo and radiation treatments. She was so weak she could hardly move. I started spending a lot more time with her. At one point I even moved into their house. We grew closer than we'd been in a long while."

Diana took a deep breath.

"Anyway, the treatments ultimately worked. She's in remission, her hair grew back and her strength has returned. This trip was meant as a welcome back present from my father to her. Once we return to New York, life will go back to normal and I will get to return to my old schedule and they will return to theirs."

David sat quietly for a moment. "I'm sorry. I assumed things about you that were completely wrong."

"Assumptions usually are," she smiled. "But thank you for saying that."

"Why?"

"I assumed that you were going to be a typical male pig. You're actually almost tolerable."

For a moment their eyes met and held for longer than they ever had before.

They moved closer together and gently kissed.

"That's disgusting," a woman's voice boomed from the entrance doorway.

They stopped kissing and looked over at an elderly couple who were staring at them with utter revulsion.

"I will be speaking to the captain about this!" the old man declared as they stomped off.

Diana and David looked to Alex for some idea as to what had upset the couple to such an irrational degree. They then saw their reflection in the mirrored wall behind the bar.

Two men stared back at them. One was masked and the other wore a pirate's bandana around his head.

Alex gave them a theatrical eye roll. Diana suddenly howled with laughter. Soon both men joined in.

It took Alex a few minutes to stop the tears from flowing down his cheeks.

"This one's definitely on me." He poured them both another pint of lager.

"May I make one rather serious observation?" David asked.

"Of course," Diana replied. "I know how important your beliefs are regarding women and their rights, but next time we kiss, if there is a next time, I would greatly appreciate if you would consider having a shave. To be perfectly honest your moustache tickles."

"I'll have to ponder that one. One kiss and suddenly you start making demands," she replied drily. "Typical man!"

David raised the new shot glass. "To us. Fuzzy face and droopy blade."

That got an even louder chuckle from Alex.

CHAPTER
FIVE

David slept fitfully. The excessive amount of alcohol that he'd ingested with Diana the previous night had knocked his internal temperature control completely out of whack. He was freezing one moment, then became so hot that sweat had soaked the sheets and pillowcase. During the occasions when he did actually sleep, he kept having one of those semi-linear dreams that seem to remain in your head for the whole night. A loose reality that doggedly reknits itself and resumes each time sleep returns.

David dreamed that he was in his old co-op building in New York where he'd lived with his ex-wife and children. He had somehow become lost after taking the wrong turn in the entry lobby. The hallways and spaces were more shiplike than reminiscent of his old building. No matter which way he tried to go he kept ending up in the Atlantic View bar. Alex greeted him warmly each time he appeared, which over the course of the night's dream sequence must have been at least twenty times. Alex seemed to know exactly what drink to prepare. He turned his back on David and after some fiddling behind the bar produced a hot mug of Ovaltine. As this had been David's favourite night-time treat as a young boy, he felt a wave of nostalgia and security.

In the dream, David asked Alex if he knew how to get back to his apartment. Alex just laughed and gave him easy instructions on how to locate apartment number 217, but would then say, "It's too late to go home now, David. This is your new home." The words terrified David in the dream. He ran out of the bar and started a new search only then to realise that he was wearing his old Winnie the Pooh pyjamas from his childhood. His surroundings became oppressively dark. He suddenly felt lost and very much alone.

By 4 a.m. he was so wrung out that he gave up trying to sleep. He was dying of thirst but didn't want to risk drinking from the tap since the salt water incident. There was also a throbbing pain behind his eyes. All in all, he felt miserable. He rarely drank to a hangover stage and felt stupid to have done so the previous night, even if he had enjoyed the experience.

He threw on some clothes and went in search of a steward who could direct him to a glass of water and a couple of Alka Seltzers.

As he walked softly down the passageway, he came across a steward's pantry area that was used for room service food prep. A steward was laying out breakfast service trays. His jacket was draped over a chair and his tie was loosened.

"Sorry to interrupt," David said.

The man jumped.

"I wasn't expecting any passengers to be up so early," he offered apologetically. "Please excuse my appearance."

He reached for his jacket.

"Please, you carry on. Don't mind me. I find myself in desperate need of an Alka Seltzer."

The steward gave him a knowing smile. "Happens to the best of us, sir."

He opened a drawer under his prep counter and revealed a veritable pharmacy. He located the requested cure-all and after pouring a glass of water, dropped two of the white discs into the clear liquid. There was a brief, uncomfortable silence while they waited for the white tablets to dissolve.

"How's Andrew doing?" David asked.

"Andrew, sir?"

"The regular cabin steward for this area," David explained.

"I don't know him, sir. I was just brought up from E Deck to take over this section."

David read his name tag. "Well, thank you, Jonah. Welcome to Main Deck."

The water in the glass had calmed. David gulped it down in one. Then helped himself to the water pitcher and refilled the glass.

"For later," he explained.

"Are you aware that the water in your cabin is completely drinkable?"

"That's actually not always the case, but thank you. You've been a life saver." David gave him a nod of thanks then headed back to his cabin. Maybe it was just wishful thinking but he felt the headache starting to abate slightly.

He thought of trying to walk some of the poison out of his system but felt he should lie down for a few minutes to let the medicine work.

He woke up five hours later.

The headache was gone but he still felt as if he'd gone ten rounds with Sonny Liston. He took an inordinately long hot shower and after carrying out his morning bathroom rituals, he realised that he wasn't feeling quite as bad.

He was then hit with a crushing realisation.

Last night was supposed to have ended with his unannounced departure from the ship. He dropped into a chair and held his head in his hands. He was disgusted with himself. Last night would have been perfect. He was completely inebriated and would most likely not have felt a thing.

He couldn't understand how someone could actually forget to kill themself.

Then, with no notice, a different thought crept into his addled mind. Had he carried through with his plan at the appointed time, what would that have done to Diana? It wasn't as if they were close. Then again, they had kissed. Did that even matter considering they were completely drunk at the time?

David couldn't seem to stop the random thoughts from cluttering up his usually disciplined mind.

One thought then crawled to the surface and dominated all others.

He was hungry.

David decided that he couldn't face the formal lunch offering in the main dining room. The brief time he'd been in the crew area, plus his bizarre dream, had made him feel slightly claustrophobic. Spending any more time that day in the bowels of the ship was to be avoided.

He stopped by the library to swap books then headed up one flight to Sun Deck. He found a private corner away from the other passengers and settled into a surprisingly comfortable deckchair.

A steward took his order for a Bloody Mary and a chicken club sandwich. His drink arrived in record time. He opened the book and started to read.

He heard the sound of another chair being dragged across the teak decking. To his dismay, it was being positioned right next to his.

He looked over to see what so-and-so had decided to invade his little corner. Diana Olson was grinning back at him. She was wearing a bright yellow sundress with oversized brass buttons and a matching hat. The colour accentuated her tanned skin. Her blue eyes sparkled as they looked into his.

"If you think you're going to be left alone up here to relax in peace, you've got another think coming. What are you reading?"

David held out the book so she could read the cover.

"Exodus! Wow – great book." She nodded her approval. "You've read it?"

"You don't have to sound so shocked. A girl can read a serious book occasionally," she replied. "Want to know the ending?"

David realised that he wasn't going to get any more reading done at that sitting. He folded a page corner over and placed the book under his deckchair.

Diana looked at him in horror. She leaned over and retrieved the book.

"How could you!" she scolded him.

She opened the book to the page he'd dog-eared and carefully straightened the fold. In exaggerated slowness, she showed him how to tuck the dustcover into the saved page.

"That's no way to treat a book," she scolded.

He looked at her in amazement. "I didn't know you were the boat's book police."

"Firstly, it's a ship, secondly, that book is from the library so it's for everyone to enjoy. Vandalising someone else's book is pretty selfish, if you ask me."

"I didn't ask you," he said.

"Then it's a good thing I happened along, isn't it?" Diana smiled.

"I forgot. You're an editor, aren't you? Protector of the written word."

"Assistant editor."

"What's the difference?" he asked.

"An office. A salary I could live on. Respect. Not having to make coffee and go out in the rain on doughnut runs. Need I go on?"

"Sorry I asked. Any chance of promotion?"

"Sure, if I suddenly grow a penis," she stated.

David wasn't sure he'd heard her correctly. One look at the cheeky expression on her face told him that he had.

"Your mother will never find you a suitable husband if you talk like that."

"Great! Penis, penis, penis!"

David looked nervously around to make sure nobody had heard her.

"Am I embarrassing you?" she teased.

"Not at all. I was worried the steward might think you were placing an order," he answered, deadpan.

Diana laughed till she had tears running down her face. David kept watching her as she tried to recover. She finally reached over and slapped him on the arm.

"You're a funny man, Mr Easton."

"Thank you, Miss Olson."

"Shame you're not the marrying kind. You could be almost bearable. With a few modifications."

"Why would you think I wouldn't want to get married?" he asked. "What modifications?"

"I knew from the second I saw you that your mind wasn't on romance. You look like someone on a mission. You're not a spy, are you?"

"If I was, I would hardly tell you, would I?" he shot back.

"What if I told you I was a spy?" Diana suggested. "Would that make it all right?"

"Totally depends who you're spying for. If you're spying for the same people I'm spying for, then maybe I could tell you. But if you're on the other side, then no. Of course, I couldn't say anything. That would be completely un-spy-like!"

"I'm not really a spy," she jokingly admitted.

"Neither am I. Then again, I would say that, wouldn't I?"

"This is getting exhausting. Would you be a darling and please order me one of those Bloody Marys?"

David flagged down a steward and ordered her drink. "Do you want a sandwich? I've got one coming."

"What did you order?" she asked.

"A chicken club," he replied.

"That sounds good. I'll have half of yours."

David looked helplessly up at the patient steward. "Just the Bloody Mary, please. By the way, have you heard anything about how Andrew is doing?"

"I'm not sure I know an 'Andrew', sir. Is he a passenger?"

"No. He's a steward. He's my cabin steward on Main Deck."

The man shook his head. "I'm terribly sorry, sir, but I don't believe I know of a steward called Andrew. Are you certain about the name?"

"It's what it says on his name badge," David replied.

"I'm afraid I can't help you there, sir. Perhaps if you were to speak with the purser, he could be of assistance to you."

The deck steward gave them both a brief smile, then left.

"That was odd," David said.

"Who's this mysterious Andrew person?" Diana asked.

"I'm sure it's nothing." He took a swig from his drink.

"I don't know about you, but I wasn't feeling one hundred per cent when I woke up this morning," she said.

"At least it sounds like you got some sleep. Every time I closed my eyes, I had dreams of mothers eating their young."

"That sounds delightful," she teased. "I took two aspirin and drank a large glass of water before going to bed. Worked like a charm."

"I though you said you felt rough this morning?"

"Of course, I did, but without the water and aspirin I would probably be bedridden."

"Sounds like you speak from experience," David quipped.

"Not at all. I just know what to do on the rare occasion I do over indulge. Speaking of which, where the hell is my Bloody Mary?"

David laughed.

"So, how do you spend your mornings, Miss Olson? I never see you around before lunchtime."

"Why do you ask? Have you been looking out for me? Have you developed feelings for me, Mr Easton?"

"No," he replied a little too quickly. "I just haven't seen you around."

"Hmmm. Well, if you must know, I have been indulging in one of the greatest luxuries of all time. I have been sleeping late followed by a scrumptious breakfast in bed. It's been absolute heaven. I then do some pleasure reading, then fit in a little work reading. By then it's midday."

"Sounds exhausting," David joked.

"What about you?" Diana said. "Perhaps you'd like to divulge what exactly you get up to in the mornings? I imagine you playing a fierce game of shuffleboard. In fact, there's a tournament today. I've already signed up."

"Are you being serious?" he asked.

"Of course. It's a fabulously athletic sport. I'd never played before this trip. Now I finally know what to do with my life, fifty years from now."

"Shuffleboard?"

"Professional level, obviously. Not that ridiculous amateur stuff," Diana replied. "Actually, that brings up a good question. Is shuffleboard actually played anywhere but at sea?"

"I hear there's a high-stakes game in Brooklyn, but you have to be invited or know someone involved," David joked.

"Perfect. I shall investigate that the moment I return."

Diana's Bloody Mary arrived. She took a sip then nibbled on the stalk of celery.

"Seriously though, where do you vanish to each morning?" Diana asked.

"Why? Have you been looking for me?"

"Not in the least. I am just a naturally curious person," she replied.

"I am, too. In fact, I'm curious as to how you know that I am not around, when you are supposedly tucked up in your bed till midday?"

"There may be the occasional morning when I'm up and about. There's just so little to do. I mean, after shuffleboard."

"If I tell you my secret, will you promise to keep it to yourself? I don't want everyone to hear about it. Once the word is out it will become the latest craze on board," David said.

"Ooh. Sounds adventurous," she said.

"Every morning, I choose some place on the ship like the engine room or the cargo hold and I set out to find it. The fun part is that I don't use the ship's guide or the signage. I have to find each target through dead reckoning."

Diana took a moment to sip her drink while studying him.

"I'm not sure if I feel the same excitement for your adventures that you obviously do," she whispered.

"That's because you've never tried it. You end up in places you never even knew existed. You see things that are really quite astounding," he insisted.

"Then I will just have to join you on your next exploration."

"I would be delighted, but there's a strict routine that goes with each day's quest."

"That's not a problem," Diana replied. "I'm quite confident that I can keep up."

"That's good to hear because, once I've completed the morning's search, I go back to my cabin and lie naked for a couple of hours while I review all that I've seen on that day's search," David advised.

Diana laughed loudly.

David stared at her with a confused look.

"I was being serious!"

Her laughter resumed. "I will only agree to the naked part if you at least wear the Zorro mask and cape."

David stared at her in wonder. She completely ignored him and focused on her drink.

Their steward arrived with the club sandwich. He had brought a second plate and cutlery so that they could share it with some degree of decorum.

They ate in silence for a while. David kept trying to catch her eye but she seemed to know exactly when he was going to try, and managed to turn her head at that moment. He wanted to see if there was anything behind her earlier wisecrack about the Zorro outfit.

"There was one thing that was rather strange during my trek yesterday morning," he said. "I was looking for the engine room and somehow stumbled upon my cabin steward being examined in the ship's infirmary."

"Are you aware how odd that statement sounded?" she said between mouthfuls.

"Now that you mention it, yes. Do you want me to go on?"

"Depends what part they were examining," she replied.

"His stomach."

"You may go on."

David couldn't help but smile. He was actually starting to like this girl. "He had the strangest rash on his stomach."

"What was strange about it? Bear in mind that I am still eating my sandwich, so please keep your reply as un-yucky as possible."

"First of all, that was my sandwich, secondly, the rash was green…"

Diana dropped what was left of her half of the sandwich onto her plate.

"Thanks a lot!"

"But it wasn't a normal green. It was greyish green with something black under it. Also, it smelled most peculiar."

"Peculiar, how?" Her interest was piqued.

"It smelled fetid – almost like decay. Something that had gone off," he continued.

"That sounds positively disgusting."

"The doctor said it was nothing to be concerned about and that aspirin and a little ointment would get rid of it," David assured her.

"Did you try to look it up in the library?" she asked.

He looked back at her, completely dumbfounded. "I was just there. I can't believe that I never even thought to look."

"And that's why men have all the good jobs." She rolled her eyes.

She rose from her deckchair and held out her hand to help him up.

"Where are we going?" he asked.

"Boy, you really are CEO material, aren't you? The library, genius. Let's go look up green funguses. Now that's what I call an exciting adventure!"

He took her offered hand.

It turned out that the ship's library had a surprisingly decent collection of medical reference books. David assumed that it was so the hypochondriac older passengers could look up their new ailments.

They found one book on rare fungi but it only dealt with those related to trees and wooded areas. They kept looking. Diana finally found one called the *Cecil Textbook of Medicine*.

It was not an easy reference book to use when you had no idea of what you were looking for. They looked up fungus and found way more types in revolting locations than they ever wanted to know about. Unfortunately, none was what David had seen in the infirmary.

They tried looking up rashes with the same result. They went through the index, word by word, to see if anything sounded likely. After almost two hours they were both exhausted and somewhat revolted by what they'd seen in the illustrations.

David went back to the shelves and had one last look around while Diana had one more scan through the textbook.

"David?" Diana called.

"I'm just checking one last row."

"David, I think you should look at this."

He could hear the concern in her voice. He returned to the table and looked over her shoulder. She had the book open on a page with a very clear photo of a large patch of greenish-black skin on a human arm.

"Oh my god," David said. "That could be it. What the hell is it?"

"Necrotic tissue. It's when areas of the body actually die."

The two stared at the picture in silence.

"Does it mention that it can be cured with ointment and aspirin?" David asked hopefully.

"It says here that necrotic means that it is dead. Once dead, it stays dead. It also says that it has the potential to keep spreading unless the dead tissue is cut away." Diana looked up at him with a worried expression.

"I think we need to go down to the infirmary this very minute and talk to the ship's doctor again. It appears he blatantly lied to me – twice."

"Perhaps it really is none of our business," she suggested.

"If my room steward is being eaten away by something they won't acknowledge – I'd say it's every bit our business."

"Do you remember the way there?"

He looked at her with surprise. "Have you forgotten who you're talking to? Exploring is my calling," David declared. "Besides, I went back there again yesterday afternoon."

"Why?"

"I wanted to check up on Andrew."

"What did he say?"

"Andrew wasn't there but I spoke to the ship's doctor."

"Was he helpful?" Diana asked.

"Actually, he was rather blunt. He said he'd released Andrew just after I saw him and that he had nothing more to do with him."

"Are you sure you want to go back down there again? It sounds to me like he doesn't want you snooping."

"I thought it was now 'us' doing the snooping?"

She rolled her eyes.

They started back in the main dining room, which was in mid service for the second lunch seating. They made their way through the crowded room and out of the same unlabelled exit. They descended the stairway but found that the door with the no entry sign was now locked.

"That's odd. This has always been unlocked," he said.

"It looks like it's meant as a subtle hint for nosy passengers," Diana suggested.

"There must be another way to get there. We could try the map, like normal people," she suggested.

"Might have to. I've got one in my room. Let's grab that one."

"Are you suggesting I come to your cabin, unescorted?"

"Are you suggesting I could be having amorous thoughts after looking at that picture of dead tissue? I may never have sex again," he said.

"That would be a shame," Diana answered coyly as she headed back up the stairs.

David followed her while desperately trying to not stare at her stunningly cute backside.

They made it up to Main Deck and David led her to his cabin. He opened the door.

"Do you think I should wait out here? What if someone were to see me go in?"

David smiled. "I think it would look far worse for you to be seen loitering in the hall outside my door."

"Good point."

She entered the room as he turned on the lights.

Diana had to stifle a scream.

Sitting in the cabin's leather armchair was the ship's doctor.

CHAPTER
SIX

"Please don't be alarmed," the doctor said calmly. "I just wanted to have a brief man-to-man conversation about this morning."

The doctor gave Diana a questioning glance.

"If you think I'm leaving, I'm not," she declared.

The doctor looked to David to do the 'right' thing.

"Sorry, Doc. She stays."

"In that case—" He reluctantly got to his feet. "I am Doctor William Aikens." He turned to Diana and held out his hand. Up close, David could see that he was older than he'd originally thought. He guessed somewhere in his early fifties. He was a heavy man and none of it looked to be muscle. He had greasy-looking hair that had receded beyond any help from his comb-over. His forehead seemed to have a sheen of oily perspiration, as if the walk to the cabin had been an ordeal.

Diana wasn't sure she wanted to shake his proffered

hand, considering what he'd been touching in the infirmary. Manners finally overtook her qualms. She shook it.

"I'm Diana Olson."

"Why don't we all sit down?" he suggested.

Diana realised that as the doctor had laid claim to the room's only chair, she would have no choice but to sit on the bed with David. In her mother's world, that would at the very least make them engaged. She was about to mention that fact when the doctor plopped himself heavily back in the chair. He let out a large sigh as the weight was taken off his legs.

She didn't have the heart to make the poor man struggle to his feet again in such a short time frame.

She sat gingerly on the edge of the bed. David sat down next to her, keeping an appropriate distance.

"I do understand your concerns about your cabin steward. I believe you have asked a number of crew members as well as myself for an update on his condition," the doctor stated.

"Yes, we have. Is there something wrong with that?" David sounded defensive.

"Normally, no. This, however, is an unusual situation. We are aboard ship in the middle of the Atlantic Ocean. There is no way for passengers to leave the vessel. The most dangerous thing that can happen mid-voyage other than fire, is panic. You asking about a crew member and alluding to his possibly being missing after observing him with a mysterious rash in the infirmary could start just such a panic. The truth, though not pleasant, is most certainly not worthy of any intrigue whatsoever."

The doctor took a moment to catch his breath.

"Your steward tipped over a coffee urn in the galley and scalded himself with boiling liquid. What you saw was a rather bad burn. I'm afraid I may have led you to believe it was far less serious than it was. Andrew is restricted to his quarters and will not be able to return to service before we dock. At that point he will receive additional treatment for the burn."

"That's awful," David exclaimed.

"The poor man. He must be in terrible pain," Diana added.

"He was initially but we have him on medication that is relieving the pain. He doesn't feel a thing. He basically just sleeps, which considering his condition, is by far the best thing."

"When I saw him in the infirmary, he didn't seem to be in any pain whatsoever and also didn't seem to be remotely drugged," David said.

"Do you have a medical background, Mr Easton?" the doctor asked casually.

"Not as such, no."

"Then please leave the armchair diagnostics to me. What you saw was a young man going into shock. His brain was masking the pain. Moments after you left, we started him on a morphine drip. Had we not, it is doubtful that the poor man would have survived."

David and Diana looked to each other for a reaction. Diana shrugged her shoulders. She had no comment.

"I thought I heard that he went back to work after I saw him in the infirmary?" David pointed out.

"I'm afraid that that little white lie was my idea. I didn't want anyone else to know about his injury," the doctor replied.

"But why?" David wouldn't let it go. "Surely telling people he'd been hurt would have been far easier and more honest than trying to conceal the whole thing."

"Mr Easton, an ocean liner has some very unusual protocols that exist in no other transportation medium. Whether anyone admits it or not, somewhere concealed inside every passenger are fears about the surrounding ocean. We are all floating within 80,000 tons of steel. Beneath us is nothing but frigid and unforgiving water.

"Fear of losing one's life while at sea is kept deep in the psyche of most passengers and is helped to stay concealed by luxury, fine food, drink and entertainment. The fact is, all of that is simply staged misdirection to ensure that the passengers' minds are occupied on pleasurable distractions rather than the possible perils that do, and always will, exist on a ship at sea. It takes very little for that dormant fear to be brought to the surface and for panic to ensue.

"The key to ensuring the stability of the illusion is through maintaining a sense of normalcy at all times. The passengers must never see any of the dirt behind the curtain. They never get to see the water sloshing in the bilge. They don't see the overcrowded crew quarters and they most certainly never see or hear about an injured crew member. That alone could be enough to cause the fragile illusion to lose some of its distractive wonder and permit a person's natural sense of fear to find its way to the surface."

Diana and David stared at the doctor in stunned silence.

"I hope you both now understand why a small measure of subterfuge may be called upon on rare occasions?"

"We had no idea," Diana voiced.

David did not seem quite as convinced. "I understand everything you've just said. But I have to ask you one more question about Andrew."

"Go on then," Doctor Williams said trying to keep the frustration out of his voice.

"If it was a nasty burn, why was it that colour? He wasn't burned by flames. He was scalded by liquid. It should have been pink or red, surely?"

The doctor reached into his white coat and brought out a white plastic tub. He opened it and held it out for the two to see.

The tub contained dark green cream and smelled foul.

"This is what you saw on Andrew's stomach. It's a mix of sulphur and aloe. It's designed to keep a burn from becoming infected while also stopping the skin from drying out." The doctor then smeared a dollop of the cream on his arm. It was definitely green.

"I hope this has alleviated your concerns," the doctor continued. "Andrew will ultimately have some disfigurement but should be able to resume his position as a cabin steward within a few months."

Doctor Aikens managed to get to his feet.

David and Diana did the same.

"I'm sorry if I caused you and the crew any trouble with my meddling. I'll put an end to that immediately," David said.

"We knew you would." The doctor gave them his best forced smile and left the cabin.

Suddenly alone in the room, the two became very conscious of their questionable moral situation.

"I'd better go and check on what my mother is up to," she declared as she headed for the door.

"Probably best." David sounded relieved.

Just before Diana closed the cabin door, she looked back and gave him a wink. "Don't think you're out of the woods yet, Mr Easton."

She shut the door leaving David mildly confused. He plopped down on the bed and tried to get his thoughts together.

David felt greatly relieved that he and Diana had not actually uncovered a shipboard conspiracy after all. Another plus was that their time together seemed to have brought them closer together. He had to kick himself as a reminder that there was no 'together' between he and Diana. What was he thinking? He didn't want to be close to anyone at the moment. He had just finished wiping his emotional slate clean. In a matter of hours, he would be dead. The last thing he needed was to start up with someone new. Especially someone like Diana. A woman who, in the right situation, he knew he could develop feelings for.

"Pull yourself together," he whispered to himself. He had no job, no home, no money and above all, no future – literally! He knew that the only reason Diana could be having any romantic thoughts for him, if she was in fact having such thoughts, was to rebel against her mother. If she knew what a complete mess his life was actually in, Diana would never have said two words to him and would be avoiding him at all costs.

He stretched out on the bed and tried to think about anything other than Diana. He failed miserably. All he could think about was her. He tried the reverse logic. He focused all his thoughts on her and fell blissfully asleep.

He dreamt he was sitting at the bar in the Plaza Hotel's famous Oak Room in New York. He was waiting for his ex-wife, Cindy, to meet him there. He had just finished work and she would have finished shopping with friends. He ordered a gin martini while he waited.

The room went quiet. He turned and saw that all the people in the bar were looking at Cindy as she walked into the room. She was wearing a bright yellow sundress with big brass buttons down the front, and an extravagantly oversized matching hat. She looked stunning. She walked over to David and kissed him tenderly on the mouth.

"I have a surprise for you," she whispered.

"Sit and have a drink and you can tell me about it," David replied as he signalled for the bartender.

Cindy produced a room key and dangled it in front of him.

"Are you sure you wouldn't prefer to come with me?" she asked in a sultry voice.

She took his hand and gently led him off the bar stool and out of the Oak Room. Once in the elevator, she began to kiss his neck. "I thought you might like a little treat."

They got out at the eleventh floor, but as they walked down the hallway, David knew that it wasn't the one from the Plaza Hotel. It was the passageway on the Main Deck onboard the Oceanis. She led him to a cabin where an open bottle of champagne was waiting on ice. She tossed her hat across the room, poured them both a glass, then downed hers in one go. She threw herself back onto the bed.

"Make love to me, David. Make love to me like you used to."

David lay beside her on the bed and began kissing her. She tasted of Cindy. The Cindy he'd loved for over twelve years. The Cindy he cheated on with a damned research assistant at work. The Cindy who'd never spoken to him again.

She kissed him back passionately. She started unbuttoning his shirt. He waited till she had finished, then started to slowly unbutton her sundress. The buttons were huge and difficult to get through the holes.

He finally undid the top four buttons and spread the yellow material apart so he could kiss her neck. He saw that she wasn't wearing a bra. He kissed the valley between her breasts as he undid another button. He moved his lips down to her stomach.

Something was wrong. Her skin didn't feel right. Also, he was conscious of an unusual odour. It smelled like rot. He looked down and saw that her entire stomach was a mottled black and green. It looked exactly like the picture in the medical reference book. Her flesh was dead.

The necrosis had eaten away her midriff and was slowly moving higher on her torso. Cindy didn't seem aware of it at all. She tried to hold him to her as he made every effort to pull away.

He finally got free and jumped to his feet. The necrosis had by then consumed her breasts and was rising up her neck. David couldn't move. He was frozen in place watching as the green and black mass reached her face. It climbed up her jaw which suddenly slackened and dropped open.

"Please, David. Make love to me like you used to." Her words were almost garbled because of her dangling jaw.

Cindy's entire face began to disintegrate. Her flesh began to fall away from her skull. Her beautiful auburn hair turned grey then white then it too fell away in clumps. Her eyes deflated into dry, shrivelled nubs.

There was little left of Cindy's face and jaw yet she asked one last time.

"Please, David. Make love to me."

David woke up shivering. It took him a few terrified moments to get his bearings and realise that he was safely in his cabin.

"Holy Christ!"

He took a drink from his bedside water glass and swung his legs off the bed.

The carpet was soaking wet.

The room suddenly tipped violently. He could hear the metal of the ship's hull plates grinding together as the liner heeled still further.

David staggered over to one of his portholes. He couldn't work out what he was seeing. The ocean was no longer ten decks below him. It was up to the level of his porthole and still rising. The top of the water rose out of his view as the ship started to tilt more quickly.

David tried to find something to hold onto but there was no hand hold. He grabbed the curtain, but as he started to fall backwards, it tore free sending him tumbling onto the floor.

The ship began to lean violently forward causing David to crumple against the side of the bed. He could clearly see

Cindy's decimated remains trying to crawl towards him from under the bed.

There was no recognisable flesh left on her skull. A greenish-grey liquid was oozing from every orifice. Her teeth had all blackened and her tongue was now jet black and as thin as a pencil. It was vibrating and seemed to be getting longer.

"Please, David. Make love to me one last time."

David woke with a start. He looked around the room and verified that there was no giant wave and most importantly, no decomposed body of his ex-wife under the bed.

He ran into the bathroom and retched into the toilet. Shaky and sweating, he turned on the cold water to splash on his face.

What came out of the tap was a dark green chunky slime.

He closed his eyes hard then reopened them. The water was clear and running freely.

David studied himself in the mirror. He wanted to make sure he was awake. He knew he was but couldn't therefore comprehend how he had just seen that stuff come out of the tap. He wondered if people could have dream flashbacks. He started to put his hands under the tap when a thought stopped him cold.

He stared at himself in the mirror. "Andrew said he had a rash. He never mentioned being burned."

The doctor had lied to them again.

CHAPTER
SEVEN

David was the first person at the velvet rope for the late dinner service. He desperately needed to speak with Diana. He wasn't sure if that would be possible at the crowded table, but he hoped they could at least make plans to meet up later.

Once permitted to enter the dining room, he made a beeline for the table. Slowly each seat was taken except the three reserved for Diana and her parents.

David heard a fuss behind him.

He turned and saw the seating steward escorting a young couple with a child who must have been about six or seven years old.

He watched in shock as they were seated in the three empty seats where until then, Diana and her parents had sat.

He tried to flag down the steward but the man rushed off to deal with the next guest issue. David left the table and caught up with him at his host station by the room's main entrance.

"Excuse me. I'm…"

"I know who you are, sir," he interrupted. "How may I help you, Mr Easton?" His tone seemed just a tad dismissive.

"The Olsons were at my table, but you seem to have sat a different family in their seats."

"I did indeed, sir."

"May I ask why?"

"I'm terribly sorry, sir, but passenger requests are considered highly confidential."

"But the daughter, Diana, was a friend," David insisted.

The steward gave him a long look. "Perhaps that was the issue, sir," the steward advised.

"May I therefore assume that you won't tell me where they have chosen to dine from now on?"

"That is correct, sir."

The steward could see the desperation on David's face.

"Are you by chance the passenger who has been trying to check up on Andrew?"

David was taken aback by the question. "Yes. I am."

The man studied him for a moment. "We were told to forget we had ever seen or known Andrew should anyone ever ask. You seem to have created quite a fuss over his disappearance and quite frankly, speaking on behalf of the crew, we're delighted. It's rare for a passenger to care about the well-being of a crew member."

He looked down at his booking chart.

"This did not come from me, but the Olsons have chosen to give up their seats in the main dining room. I believe they plan to use the Veranda Grill as their dining option."

"But why? Diana and I were just getting close," David replied.

"Sir, if I may be so direct – I believe you have just answered your own question."

The steward had to focus on another couple that had a complaint about their seating assignment.

David walked back to his table. After finally getting over the sense of frustration at losing Diana as a table mate, he ended up having a very pleasant dinner. Ron Stanford told a bizarre story about the days when he ran a cathouse on the east coast. Apparently, he used to ferry the young women to their appointed clients in a massive Cadillac while completely inebriated. His wife, Wendy, looked on with an expression of mild embarrassment, as her husband regaled them with his tawdry tales. The young couple with the child looked horrified.

David couldn't help wondering why the ship's doctor had lied about Andrew's injuries. Unless there really was a conspiracy concerning the cause of his ailment. What if David had actually seen a case of some horrifically contagious disease that would infect the entire ship?

He tried to brush such thoughts away as they were way too incendiary and besides, if they thought it was highly contagious, they would hardly have been standing over the man staring at the infection site without any protection whatsoever. They would have at the very least worn masks. Wouldn't they?

The dinner ended with the ship's mid-voyage dinner specialty. Once the main course had been consumed and the table cleared of glasses and plates, two stewards lowered a flaming Baked Alaska to the centre of the table.

The flames rose up the side of the whipped egg-white mountain, charring the white peaks to blackened points. David's mind flashed back to the necrotic wound. As the others at the table marvelled over the sight of the glorious dessert, David felt his stomach do a back flip.

David excused himself and headed back to his cabin. He suddenly felt quite nauseous, while at the same time oddly emotional. He felt as if he was about to scream but had no idea why. He reached his cabin door and with a shaky hand, inserted the key. The moment he turned the door handle, someone pushed him from behind, then entered the room uninvited.

David was about to strike out at the attacker when Diana told him to shush. She quietly closed his door then turned on the cabin lights.

"Sorry about that. I've been lurking around the service pantry waiting for you to get here," she explained breathlessly.

David turned to face her.

"My god! You look awful. What happened?" she asked.

"It's been a strange day," he said as he plopped down into the leather chair. "I should ask you the same question."

"You mean I look awful?"

"No. I meant what's happened to bring you down to my cabin?"

"Apparently, one of my mother's shipboard cronies saw us together on deck this afternoon. As it was told to her, we looked to be having an intimate conversation and our body language displayed lustful ambition."

David looked back at her in amazement. "You're joking, right? First of all, who the hell talks like that. We're not in the 1920s. Secondly, we were just having a drink and a sandwich. There was no lust."

"You sure about that?" she asked with a big smile.

"Well, maybe there was a little lust but surely it wasn't enough to report back to your mother," David replied.

"Well, my mother thought it was valuable information and determined that I wasn't to be seen with you anymore."

"But there was nothing going on. What has she got against me?" David was getting angry.

"My mother feels that none of the big game will focus on the poor gazelle if there's already a lion stalking it."

"You're the gazelle?"

She nodded.

"And I'm the lion?"

She nodded again.

"Cool. I always wanted to be a lion," David grinned. "Aren't you risking a lot by sneaking down here like this?"

"Nothing that I don't mind losing."

It took a moment for the double meaning to sink into David's caveman brain.

"I don't think you really want to be with me. Nor should you. You know nothing about who I am. If you did, you'd run right out of this cabin and never give me another glance."

"Okay then," Diana said. "Do your best. Tell me these great horrors of yours that would send me screaming back to my parents."

Diana sat in the chair and watched as David mulled over his options. He finally decided to give the truth a try.

"Okay. So, in chronological order, I had an affair then my wife divorced me. My father-in-law fired me, then blackballed me. My ex won't let me see my kids. And finally, I am completely broke, as I spent everything I had on this voyage so I could throw myself off the ship within the next day or so."

Diana studied him carefully, then started laughing.

"I'm being completely serious," he stated.

"I'm sure you are," she replied. "However, my dear, you are simply going through a rough patch, albeit a bad one. I have no doubt in my mind that you will get another job…"

"But…" David tried to interrupt.

"Shush! I'm talking at the moment. If for some reason you find it impossible to get a decent job in New York, then move. Clearly the city doesn't exactly hold much magic for you anymore. Try Chicago or Los Angeles. You'll get to actually start over. Do you know how many people dream of being able to do that?"

"But…"

"Still not finished," she smiled. "As for your dramatic suicide plans – I give you full marks for initiative but zero for completion. If you were that intent on ending your life, you could have jumped out of your apartment window in New York. What floor do you live on?"

"The twelfth," David replied reluctantly.

"Perfect. You would have had to go head first to be sure to make a good splat on the sidewalk. Oh, and you definitely would have had to avoid any shop awnings, but it would have most certainly been fatal and quick. Then there's the subway and there's any number of bridges. The list goes on and on. Yet you choose a date far enough in the future so that circumstances could actually change. And, in case you haven't noticed, they have changed."

"How have they changed?" David voiced. "Okay – let's say I did agree that I could move to a new city and start over. I have literally no money. I spent it all. I have a one-way ticket to Southampton. I couldn't even get back if I wanted to. Besides, despite what you think about my dedication to this plan, I still have every intent of diving off this fabulous ship and sinking down into the great abyss."

"You sound like you are reciting something from a play or something?" Diana shook her head. "Let's just for fun be a smidge pragmatic. So, you go to the stern of the ship one blustery night. You manage to stand on the fantail railing, then jump…"

"Dive…" he corrected.

"Okay, dive. And I assume, in your fantasy, you enter the water like a knife, then glide down to the dark depths and gently fade away."

"Something like that," he replied.

"Let me give you the more realistic image of your grand exit. You get to the fantail and are freezing. The spume from the ship ploughing through the rough sea has coated the deck and railings. It's slippery. You become soaked to the skin and start shivering. You somehow manage to climb the railing and try to swing a leg over to the other side. You slip and end up with your leg trapped between the stanchions, as you dangle over the stern directly above the propeller wash."

She stopped and checked his expression. David had gone a few shades paler.

"You try to release your leg but it's really stuck. You finally manage to free it and attempt to hoist yourself back to a more dignified position so you can perform this great swan dive of yours. Your foot slips on the wet metal safety lines and you fall directly into the prop wash. You instantly find yourself in a maelstrom. You can't get your breath, however that doesn't matter. You are sucked into the vortex caused by the starboard propeller. You are lucky. The blade only slices off your left arm before the force of the water forces you back into the ship's wake. You try to stay afloat, but with one arm, it's almost impossible. You are losing blood at a horrific rate. You are getting woozy. You want it to end but you can't seem to sink yourself fully." Diana notices his palor.

"Are you all right?" she asked.

David looked back at her with an expression of dread. He managed to nod half-heartedly.

"You find that by lying flat on your back, you are able to float. You decide to stay in that position until the blood loss takes away your last breath. Unfortunately, all that blood has not gone unnoticed. You have attracted sharks. At first, they just circle you and explore. Then the first one takes a bite of your leg. The second, a much larger shark, takes your other leg off at the knee. You are now screaming in agony. The sharks are now in full frenzy and rip your body apart, one piece at a time. You are alive for most of their attack. That, dear David, is the more likely outcome of your grand exit strategy. What do you think about the romantic vision of your suicide plan now?"

David tried to look blasé about it, then clasped his hand over his mouth and ran into the bathroom and started throwing up.

Diana sat cross-legged on the bed, smiling to herself. She was pretty sure that she had given David a whole new outlook on his life, and especially his poorly thought-out suicide scenario.

David eventually returned looking pale and embarrassed.

"That was disturbingly graphic."

"That was the whole point," Diana replied. "You'd conjured up some romantic notion of suicide that was nothing but fantasy. I had to shock you out of such a ludicrous idea."

"Wanting to kill myself was not ludicrous," he argued. "It was the only choice I had."

"Do you see what you just did? You said **was** and **had.** In other words, you used the past tense. I don't think you actually want to kill yourself anymore. If indeed you ever did," she insisted.

"You realise you're taking all the fun out of my suicide, don't you?"

"Good. That was my intent."

"Why, though?" David asked. "It's not like you really care about me. What difference would it make if I were suddenly gone?"

Diana gave that a moment's thought.

"I would forever wonder if that nice man I'd started to get to know could have become something special in my life."

Their eyes met. Diana's were filled with enthusiasm. David's, with doubt.

"Please don't say things like that to me just to try and help. I have never in my life been as lonely as I have over the last year. Hearing you say those words…"

David stopped to get his emotions in check.

"Hearing you say those words seems completely impossible to me. I have fallen into such a dark place that the thought of someone actually caring has become inconceivable and therefore, unbelievable."

"Last night, after you let your guard down…" Diana began.

"You got me drunk!"

"Whatever. Once you'd let your guard down I could see through that barrier you'd managed to build around yourself. I had a glimpse of David from before all that ugliness occurred. We had fun, so please take it from me that having someone interested in you is both conceivable and believable. I am the living proof of that. You're just going to have to stay alive and deal with it. And me."

He studied her for a long time.

"I suppose I could hold off for a while and see where all of this takes us," he announced with renewed enthusiasm.

"That-a-boy!" She grinned. "How about you pulling yourself together and us grabbing some dinner. I'm starving."

"I'm not sure we can be seen together in any of the public spaces while your mother is on the warpath. Besides, I ate dinner already at the table you and your family decided was no longer suitable."

"You know perfectly well that that was never my idea. I look forward to our dinner banter," Diana said. "Would you think it highly indecent of me to suggest that we order some cocktails and a snack here in your cabin? It may just be the only choice. With my mother on the warpath, I think it would be much safer at this point for us to stick to room service."

"For the rest of the trip? That would certainly turn a few heads." Even as he said the words, he had a mental flash of his recent dream with Cindy's fleshless skull trying to form words.

"No, silly. Just for those emergencies when we have nowhere else to go."

"Go ahead. Order whatever you want," he gestured to the phone.

Diana gave him a disbelieving look. "You do realise that a woman ordering martinis from your cabin would most definitely get the staff jungle drums going? It would be ship-wide gossip before the martinis even arrived."

"Doesn't it worry you that you always seem to be right?"

"Not in the least," she smiled.

"I guess I should make the call," he replied.

"Clever boy."

David ordered two martinis and a steak sandwich with French fries. Diana was making urgent hand gestures that had something to do with scooping. He finally caught on and added a portion of vanilla ice cream.

When he hung up the phone, Diana was pretending to look displeased.

"What?" David asked.

"Vanilla? I was doing an impression of a peach."

He gave her a stern glare.

"I guess, considering the unusual situation, vanilla will do very nicely," she added.

"We have a while," he said. "Tell me more about you. You certainly now know enough about my train wreck of a life."

"May I use your—" She gestured to the bathroom.

"Of course. It's a bit of a mess."

"I won't look if you promise not to listen," she bargained.

She walked into the bathroom. David heard her first lock the door, then turn both the sink and bath taps on to mask any sound. He couldn't help but smile.

She was back in record time. She sat back down on the edge of the bed and gave David a raised-eyebrow expression.

"What?" he asked.

"I realised in there that you had told me hardly anything about yourself. That was very sneaky. Just giving me the last year or so, hoping for sympathy."

"I wondered if you'd pick up on that," David smiled.

"Go on then."

"Fine. Here you go. I was born…"

"Too much. Just the good bits, please," Diana interrupted.

"Sorry." He started over. "I was raised in Fairfax, Virginia. I was and still am absolute crap at all sports. I had an affinity for the sciences, especially biology. I ended up getting a scholarship at a university to study molecular biology. I eventually got my PHD then landed the job in New York."

"Slow down a minute," Diana said. "Which university?"

"It doesn't matter."

"Yes, it does. I'm still in the evaluating phase with you. Impress me."

"Harvard," David mumbled.

"I couldn't hear you," she pushed.

"Harvard!" he boomed.

Diana grinned. "Better. So, I get the fact that you're a science guy but I haven't heard yet about your love life back then."

"You haven't heard about it because there wasn't one. I was too busy studying and researching to have time for a social life."

"There must have been someone?" Diana asked.

David took a long breath, dreading having to answer her question.

"Cindy. That's my ex-wife. She was my first."

"Your first what?"

"My first everything. My first real date. My first real kiss. My first… you know." He stared down at his feet.

"Are you telling me you married the first girl that let you kiss her!?" She was actually surprised.

"Basically, yes."

"Then no wonder you had an affair." Diana laughed. "You were just catching up."

"I know how pathetic that makes me sound," David added.

"Actually, it makes you sound kind of sweet."

"Okay, I've told you about me."

"So, it's my turn?" Diana tried to sound coy.

David nodded. Diana took a moment to gather her thoughts.

"I was born into a…"

"Just the highlights, please," he grinned.

"I think my birth is a huge plot point." She tried to keep a straight face.

David sighed.

"Okay, then. Just the milestones. I'm now twenty-nine.

I grew up in Connecticut. At eleven, my mother decided that I needed to go to finishing school, so I was packed off to Switzerland."

"What in God's name is a finishing school?" David asked.

"It's supposed to be where young girls become young ladies. We were taught elocution, deportment and all the other social graces. You know the stuff I mean."

"Pray tell – why did your mother think you needed all that? It sounds a bit archaic."

"It was," Diana agreed. "But my mother believed it was the proper thing to do. I couldn't come out as a debutante without a full understanding of social graces, could I?" she explained.

"You were a debutante?" David sounded amazed. "I would have loved to have seen that."

She gave him a sneer.

"I never said I was. I said my mother was training me to be one. The fact was that I thought the whole thing was nuts. I wasn't going to dress up in some hideous ball gown and be displayed with all the other new debutantes just so the male spawn of Manhattan's wealthiest families could decide whether I was good enough for them. I may as well have been a one-year-old colt being paraded around before a horse auction."

"Minus the ball gown," David quipped.

"Obviously." She tried not to smile. "Anyway, I went to the Swiss school. They showed me how to walk, how to talk, how to speak languages – everything a finely bred young lady needs to know."

"Was your mother pleased with the end results?"

"God, no," she grinned. "I refused to listen to a word they were trying to teach me in Switzerland. I became a rebel. I was finally asked to leave the school after only two terms. I think it was a record. From then on, I basically turned into a tomboy and disappointed my parents at every turn. Unfortunately, my mother refused to give up on the hope that she can still coerce some nice wealthy gentleman into marrying her poor wanton daughter."

"Wanton?"

"A little," she replied.

"How little?" David asked.

"Anyway – as I was trying to say, after the whole Swiss thing, they gave it one more try and packed me off to Vassar College. I gave the boys a wide berth and focused on studying communications and creative writing. I already knew that I wanted to be an editor. I just wasn't sure what type. I started writing spec articles about women's interests, especially stories about women who excelled in their specific field. Amazingly, some were published. The magazine where I now work started giving me assignments while I was still in college. After commencement, they offered me an intern position. Two years later they gave me a real job earning real money."

"Enough to live on?" David asked.

"Of course not. I was still a woman, after all."

"What did your family think of you holding down a job instead of holding down a husband?"

"Do you wish to rephrase that?" she smiled.

"No, thank you. I liked the clever wording."

She punched him in the arm.

"So that's pretty much my life in a nutshell," she announced.

"What about men?" David asked.

"What about them?" she replied.

"There didn't appear to be any in your story."

"None were worthy of mention in my redacted history."

"No serious relationships?"

"If you mean, have I ever had sex then the answer is yes. I'm twenty-nine. It's 1962. I hope that doesn't eliminate me from consideration."

"Consideration for what?" he asked pointedly.

"That remains to be seen."

There was a loud knock on the cabin door. Panic immediately ensued. Diana straightened the bed cover, grabbed her belongings, then dashed into the bathroom all in one fluid motion. David waited until he'd got his breathing under control then opened the door.

A steward held a serving tray, one handed at shoulder height. David stepped aside to let him in. He rested the tray on the cabin's tiny writing desk, retrieved a folding suitcase stand from the hanging cupboard, then placed the dinner tray upon it. He pointed out each item to confirm it was as ordered.

Once done, David tipped him a dollar. As the steward walked past the closed bathroom door, he asked in a professional tone, "Do you need anything else, madam?"

Diana opened the door. "How did you know?"

The steward smiled. "Miss, you were lying in wait for over thirty minutes in one of our most used service pantries. We left you in peace and worked from another one further down the hall. If I may suggest – next time you feel the need for subterfuge, that you not use quite such a potentially busy hideout."

David stepped over and gave the man another dollar.

"Sorry for the inconvenience," David said. "May I ask one other thing, while you are here?"

"Of course, sir."

"What have you heard about my previous cabin steward – Andrew? Do you know what actually happened to him?"

The steward suddenly looked nervous.

"Is everything all right?" Diana asked. "You seem uncomfortable."

"We've been told to not discuss that issue with anyone. Especially not with passengers," he replied in a lowered voice.

"I only want to know if he's going to be all right?" David explained.

The steward looked to Diana then back to David.

"We were told that he's already been disembarked. He was transferred to a sister ship that was on a course back to New York."

"You mean he was transferred at sea?" David asked.

"Yes, sir."

"Is that even possible?" Diana asked.

"Yes. It is." The steward took a deep breath. "So long as both ships can either stop or run parallel at a very slow speed, it's perfectly safe. It happens more often than you would imagine."

"I'm not aware that either occurrence has taken place,"

David said. "Have we stopped or slowed in the last few days?"

"Not that I'm aware of, sir." The steward's response was almost a whisper. "However, I mainly work below deck, so I would most likely not be aware of such an occurrence anyway."

The three stood in silence by the cabin door.

"Well, then – thank you for bringing us our dinner," David voiced.

"It was a pleasure, sir, madam. However, I only brought dinner for one." He gave them a subtle wink then turned and exited the room.

Diana and David stood staring at the closed cabin door.

"Well, that was odd," Diana remarked.

"What exactly have they done with poor Andrew?" David added.

"I somehow doubt they could hide him away successfully without someone from the crew spotting him," she said.

Someone began banging on the door. David gestured for Diana to stay silent.

"Who's there?" David shouted in a gruff voice.

"This is Mrs Arthur Olson and I demand you open your door."

David shoved Diana into the bathroom then before shutting the door, mouthed, "Don't come out for any reason."

Once the door was firmly shut, he undressed completely then opened the cabin door, keeping it between the angry woman in the passageway and his nude body.

"What can I do for you, Mrs Olson?" he asked.

"I want to speak to my daughter immediately – and what are you doing hiding behind that door?"

"Your daughter isn't here and I am hiding so as to not upset you. I am naked, you see."

"I know my daughter is in there. I have it on good authority that she waited for you in one of the pantries," she stated with authority.

"I haven't seen your daughter tonight, Mrs Olson, as you went out of your way to change your dinner seating," David said.

"I demand that you let me in this cabin this minute!" Diana's mother insisted.

"Very well then." He stepped out from behind the door enabling him to open it fully. David then stood facing her, his nude body in plain view.

Diana's mother gasped and staggered backwards. "How dare you."

"How dare me? How dare you, madam. I was asleep in my bed when you roused me, then insisted I admit you to my private quarters despite having told you that I was completely naked. There's only one person at fault here and it certainly isn't me!"

Her face had turned beetroot red as she tried to get her words out.

"I will inform the captain of this," she stammered.

"And tell him what? That I dared be naked in the privacy of my own room?"

"You permitted me to see you like that intentionally."

"You're of course completely right, Mrs Olson. I've been plotting this since the first moment I came aboard. It's been my obsession to have you try and break down my cabin door and then see me naked."

"You are a disgusting man!" She turned and stumbled down the hall.

"And don't think I didn't notice how many times you glanced at me below the waist," he called after her.

The steward from earlier chose that minute to walk by the cabin. He saw Mrs Olson clomping away and David standing naked by his open door. He tried but failed to conceal a laugh.

"Nicely done, sir."

He kept on walking.

David closed the door. Before he could get dressed, Diana stepped out of the bathroom. She looked at him from top to bottom.

"I could work with that."

She blew him a kiss then opened the door a crack. She saw that the passageway was clear.

"Where are you going?" David asked. "Your dinner's here."

"Not the right time. I have every faith in my mother that she may well get the captain involved. I don't want to be here when a search party arrives."

She slipped into the hall. David was about to close the door when he had a thought. "How do I find you tomorrow?"

"I'll find you." She closed the door on him.

David returned to the cabin's only chair and stared at the tray the steward had delivered. They hadn't had a chance to attack the martinis or the sandwich before Diana's psychotic mother had assaulted his cabin door.

He lifted the silver plate cover and smiled.

"I don't suppose there's anything wrong with having two dinners."

Still stark naked, he settled himself into the armchair as he downed the first martini in one giant gulp.

CHAPTER
EIGHT

David managed to finish his second dinner, including the ice cream and both martinis. He was feeling pretty good about the world at that moment. He had donned a terrycloth robe and was lounging on the bed when he heard someone trying to open his cabin door. A key turned in the lock and two men walked into his room. They didn't look like passengers or, for that matter, crew. These guys were big. Both wore black trousers and black T-shirts. Their heavily muscled arms were in plain view.

The men stared down as David tried to swing his legs off the bed.

"Stay where you are, Mr Easton," one of the men commanded. "This won't take long if you play it right."

"I don't know who you are, but you have no right…" David tried to sound threatening.

"We got every right. So please shut the hell up," the other man interrupted.

David realised that both men sounded distinctly like New Yorkers. The Bronx, to be specific.

"We are here to deliver you a message," the first one said. "You've been nosing around things that don't concern you. 'Cause of that, we've been asked to pay you a courtesy visit. We hope that this will be the only visit necessary 'cause if there's another one, it won't be so courteous. You get what I'm saying here?"

David nodded. "Who are you guys? Do we have marines on board?"

The men laughed coldly.

"We ain't no marines," the first one said. "We work below decks doing the heavy lifting for the engineering guys. Occasionally we do some heavy work on the higher decks when there's a passenger that we're told needs a courtesy visit."

"I don't need a visit of any kind," David insisted.

"That's not what we were told," number two replied. "You and your little girlfriend need to mind your own business and just enjoy the trip like everyone else. Am I making myself clear?"

"Completely," David nodded.

"That's good to know. We got better things to do than come up here and break bones," number one advised.

"We're gonna leave you now, Mr Easton. Enjoy the rest of your evening," number one said as he glanced over at the empty martini glasses.

They both gave him a creepy smile then turned and left the cabin.

David lay on his bed afraid to move. He was terrified that they might change their minds and return for some of that 'breaking bones' they'd threatened him with.

He suddenly felt intensely claustrophobic. The walls of his first-class cabin seemed to be closing in on him. Despite his earlier martini guzzling, he suddenly had a craving for another drink. Somehow the nice buzz he'd got from the cocktails had completely vanished.

He tidied himself up and headed to the Neptune Cocktail Lounge two decks below the bridge. It had only just gone midnight so he hoped the place would still be quite busy. He felt he needed the safety of a crowd in his favourite onboard watering hole.

He walked forward to one of the ship's grand staircases then made his way up to the next deck. He crossed the ornate stairway lobby and passed through a pair of stunning, hand-etched, Lalique glass doors. The Neptune Cocktail Lounge was even more spectacular at night. It was decorated in an authentic yet subdued art deco style. The bar was a half-circle that ran almost from the port to the starboard side of the vessel.

Opposite the bar, facing forward, was that incredible view. The floor to ceiling windows that ran the entire width of the room were even more dramatic in the evening. As you drank your cocktail, you could look out over the illuminated bow and foredeck and see the raging ocean beyond. At least you could on a clear day. That night you could only just make out the bow through the dense fog. The sodium lights lit up the grey mist as it swirled and eddied around the foredeck loading crane.

David was surprised to see that there was an empty table for two right in front of one of the windows. He made straight for it and sank into a black studded leather armchair.

A steward appeared almost immediately. David ordered a large Courvoisier. He stared out at the front of the mighty ship and the complete greyness beyond. He sensed someone approaching his table. He turned away from the window expecting to see his steward. Instead, he watched Diana's father plop down in the leather chair across from him.

"One doesn't often get to see a sight like that, does one?" Mr Olson asked.

David was at a loss for words. He finally mumbled a weak, "No." Mr Olson turned from the window and looked David in the eye. "We seem to have ourselves a little problem, don't we, son?"

David desperately wished that his brandy had already been delivered. He tried to come up with the right words but the other man continued.

"First of all, I owe you an apology for my wife's actions. As you may have noticed, she can sometimes be wound up just a little too tightly. Don't get me wrong, she can be as sweet as punch most of the time but nothing drives her crazier than when she's trying to match-make for Diana. It's like she's got a pair of blinkers on. All rationality seems to go out of the window. I'd say banging on your door at eleven at night would be a prime example."

The steward arrived with David's drink. He set it down on an embossed coaster then placed a small crystal bowl of olives and another with potato chips on the table between the two men.

"May I get you anything, sir?" he asked Mr Olson.

Arthur looked to David. "What are you having?"

"A large Courvoisier."

Arthur smiled up at the steward. "I'll have the same. Thank you."

The steward headed back to the bar, leaving them on their own again.

"David – may I call you David?"

David nodded.

"David, my daughter is a spirited woman. She has a mind of her own and does exactly what she wants, when she wants. Her mother thinks she is still a virgin and is about to enter spinster territory. Nothing could be further from the truth. She has a great life in New York, a career that she loves and the brains to make the most of it, but only on her terms. Poor Myra, that's her mother, she still believes that she will find Di the perfect man. They'll fall madly in love, Diana will quit her job and make a bunch of grandchildren that Myra can dote over."

"I don't see that as being Diana's number one priority, Mr Olson," David offered.

"Call me Arthur. You know – you are absolutely right. Di is going to do what she feels is best for her. I don't see anyone being able to derail that girl. My problem is that Myra just won't accept any part of that scenario. For the sake of a relatively peaceful marriage, I pretend to go along with her, but there are times when I have to do some fancy footwork behind the scenes. This is one of those times. I might be getting on a bit, but I can still see what's as clear as the nose on my face. Diana likes you. I'm not gonna read any more into it than she's made a friend. What you both do beyond that is up to you. I just have to find a way of getting Myra to accept that fact and to give you both some space."

Arthur stopped talking as the steward placed his brandy before him along with another bowl of olives and one of potato chips.

He raised his snifter to David. "Cheers, young man."

"Cheers, sir."

They both took a sip of their drinks.

"There's one thing you don't know about me, David. I am very fair but at the same time, very pragmatic. I want Diana to be happy, but I also don't want her getting conned by some shipboard lothario who's either after a quick lay, or worse, wants to weasel his way into the heart of a girl with a sizeable trust fund."

David wasn't sure how to respond. "I didn't know she had a trust fund, sir."

"I believe you, David. I sent a wire to New York the moment I saw a spark between you two at our first dinner together. I wanted to know who you were. Wanted to make sure you weren't some wolf hiding in plain sight."

"Should I start running now?" David asked.

Arthur let out a veritable roar of laughter. Heads turned throughout the bar. "I learned a lot about you. You were never a wolf. I was kind of surprised to learn that you're a research microbiologist."

"Was a research microbiologist."

"I was even more intrigued when I heard that you'd lost your wife, your home and your job."

"Correct again, sir," David added with growing concern.

"I also heard that you've found it impossible to find another position in New York. Well, let me tell you something, David. The world is a very strange place.

People say they don't believe in coincidences, but I personally think those people just aren't paying attention. Let me give you an example. Your father-in-law was Lionel Messer. His daughter, Cindy, is your ex-wife."

David realised that he had eaten all the potato chips in his bowl while listening, spellbound by the other man's words. Arthur pushed his bowl over to him and continued.

"Twenty years ago, I started my first pharmaceutical company. I had a financial partner – the one and only Lionel Messer. Let me tell you about that man. He is a weak, conniving, untalented little crook. I caught him skimming from the company. He was cooking the books as they say, from day one. He'd created a fictitious supply company which delivered exactly nothing yet were paid close to half a million dollars. I of course had my lawyers dissolve the partnership immediately but I decided not to have him prosecuted. The condition was that he had to pay back everything he'd taken and he had accepted the fact that I would be keeping a close eye on his business practices. I also reminded him that I had all the documentation I needed to have him behind bars if he ever tried to cross me or anyone else again."

"Oh my god!" David stammered.

"I know. Coincidence, right?"

"I'd say so."

"There's more. Your sweet wife, Cindy – she divorced you for having an affair with your research assistant. Well, son, there's a little bit more to it than that. At the time she accused you of infidelity, Cindy was two years into her own affair. For what it's worth, she's still living with the guy. Anyway, she wanted to find a way to get rid of you without making herself the brunt of a scandal. What better way than to make you look like a cheating schmuck. She had her daddy place that assistant in your department and offered her a handsome bonus if she could seduce you."

"That's not possible. Nobody could be that calculating."

"Son, did I not mention that the man is a crook? You, unfortunately, fell for the bait, which would normally have put you in my bad books, but I'm pretty sure that you didn't have much choice. I'm betting that dear Cindy stopped providing you with her wifely attentions and any modicum of respect at some point many months earlier. That cessation of physical affection mixed with what I would consider to be complete lack of respect was timed perfectly. When a beautiful woman at work became interested in you and started telling you how wonderful you were, you took the worm and swallowed the whole damn hook. That about right?"

David looked at the other man with growing respect and amazement. "Pretty much dead on," David nodded.

"You should know that less than an hour ago I sent two additional wires. One was to Lionel Messer, reminding him of our little clandestine relationship. He may have his own successful company now, but his past dealings could bring that tumbling down in less time than it would take me to make a couple of phone calls. I told him to un-blackball you as well as pay you your back salary from the day he fired you. The second wire was to my business affairs VP. He is going to make sure that every major pharmaceutical research company in New York is going to know that you are available for employment effective immediately. They will further know that I would consider it a great favour were you to be hired by one of those companies."

"But, sir – why? I'm not your son-in-law? I have no idea whether Diana and I will become..."

"Dear boy, please don't misconstrue my actions as having anything to do with Diana whatsoever. You both can do whatever you're going to do. I don't care. My actions were solely based on you having been treated entirely unfairly by someone I truly despise. You gave me the unusual opportunity of making a magnanimous gesture on one hand, while being able to turn the knife in a man I loathe with the other."

"I don't know what to say." David was actually moved by what Arthur had done.

"There's one more little thing I had my guy do. I hope you won't mind. He's going to advise a friend of mine who just happens to be the district attorney for New York, all about the plot that Lionel and Cindy hatched. Your divorce will be reviewed, especially your alimony and custody rights. As I believe that Cindy may soon be spending some time in state custody, I think you'll find that you will be able to have much more time with your kids, if you decide you want to spend time with them. From what I hear they're a couple of little terrors."

Arthur was stunned to see that David was holding a hand over his mouth as his eyes began to mist over.

"I hope those are tears of joy, son?"

David nodded. "They are, sir. They surely are."

"Then that's all right."

Both men took a moment to enjoy their drinks and stare out at the ship's bow as it gently rose and fell in time with the ocean swell.

"There's one small additional thing which as a dutiful husband, I have to request. I would consider it a huge favour to me personally, if you would refrain from flashing your private parts at my wife for the duration of this voyage. She was so horrified, I had to give her something to calm her down when she returned to our suite."

"Sorry about that, sir. I give you my word that I will never again expose myself to your wife."

"I hope that's a sentence you rarely have to use, David."

"I would truly like to believe that this will be the first and last time, sir."

"Good to hear."

They sat in the bar for over an hour talking about real estate, New York, food – just about everything. They finally called it a night at 1 a.m. and headed back to their respective cabins.

David returned to Main Deck and started down the long corridor to his room. He passed a partially open cabin door and couldn't help but glance in. He saw the doctor and ship's captain standing by a man seated in a chair. The man was crying.

He was naked save for a pair of white briefs. His entire body had been consumed by the greenish-black necrosis. Only his head was so far unaffected. The man didn't seem to be in pain. He was just crying out of fear.

As David watched, the necrosis crept up his neck and then face. It reached his hairline then completely engulfed his head. David couldn't take his eyes off the horrific sight.

He watched as the edges of the man began to diffuse. His entire profile started to dissolve into a greenish powder that rode the air until it disappeared entirely. Within only a few seconds, there was nothing left of him. Not a trace except for the pair of white briefs.

David moved quickly away from the door before the doctor and captain could see him. He had no idea that he had just witnessed the second person on board ship succumb to the green plague.

CHAPTER
NINE

David slept fitfully. He kept seeing the poor man disintegrate in front of his eyes. He felt he should tell someone. Then again, the best person to tell had been standing only a few feet away from the horror. The captain was clearly aware of what was going on. He was also in a far better position to know what to do in such a situation.

Besides, David was still reeling from the two thugs that had threatened him with bone breaking. There was only one person he could talk to about it and he had no idea where he could find her.

He heard the daily journal slide under his door and retrieved it, wondering if there would be anything written about the mysterious goings-on. There wasn't. It was almost identical to the previous day's rag. Fog, mild temperatures and calm seas. The only differences were that shuffleboard had been replaced with a deck tennis competition and the clay-pigeon shooting had been cancelled until the fog lifted.

David did his mandatory three laps of the promenade deck then, after a quick bath, joined the breakfast throng waiting for the velvet rope to be removed.

He felt someone tap him on the shoulder causing him to actually jump.

"Steady there, David," Diana smiled. "It's only me. I hoped I'd find you down here. I had the seating steward put me back on your table."

"What about your mother?"

"She and Daddy had a talk late last night. I'm not certain exactly what was said, but it was decided that I could eat where and with whom I chose."

"Wow. That's a surprise," David said.

"Is it, though?"

"What does that mean?"

"I know you had drinks with my father last night. Then this morning I'm permitted to actually see you. You didn't ask him for his blessing, did you? Are you about to propose, David? Oh, please say you are. I haven't had a good proposal in months," Diana grinned.

Before he could say anything, the red rope was removed and the waiting diners surged like cattle heading for fresh grass.

Neither Diana nor David were particularly hungry. David played with a poached egg and Diana with a slice of wheat toast. They wanted to talk, but there was no chance of privacy at the crowded table.

They finally gave up on the food and went up to the open-air sports deck. The fog seemed even heavier than on previous days. They walked to the area directly behind the number one funnel and sat on a slightly damp bench.

"I saw another one," David stated. "Another person with necrosis."

"How bizarre. Was he as bad as the steward?" Diana asked.

"I think it's fair to say that he was substantially worse."

"How awful. Was he in the infirmary?"

"No. He was in a cabin on the same deck as me," he said. "About ten doors down from mine."

"Why wasn't he in the infirmary?" she asked.

"I doubt there was time," David stated.

"What does that mean?" she prodded. "Did he die?"

"He did more than that. He disintegrated into the air. He just dissolved."

Diana gave him a long, concerned look.

"That sounds like one of your strange dreams."

"I wish it had been a dream," he voiced. "The sad fact is – it was actually real. The necrosis was spreading while I watched. It went up his neck, then face, then – poof. He was gone."

"Did you try to help?" she asked.

"How? This wasn't something anyone could stop. It happened really fast," David said.

"How do you know that it couldn't be stopped? You're not a doctor."

"I'm not, but the ship's doctor and the captain were standing next to him watching the whole thing."

"And neither tried to help? The man's screaming must have been horrific."

"He didn't scream," David explained. "He was crying. He seemed to know what was happening and just accepted it."

"This is complete nonsense. We are going down to the infirmary right this minute. I want to have another word with that doctor."

David took a deep breath before continuing. "We can't."

"Of course we can. As passengers we have a perfect right to know what's going on on board this ship. Especially when you've witnessed a strange death. How do we know it's not contagious? There have been two instances already. Whatever this is could contaminate everyone on board. I have no intention of just sitting around waiting for that to happen."

"After you snuck out of my cabin last night, a couple of crewmen stopped by to say hello."

"Why?" she asked.

"They were sent by the doctor to give me what they referred to as a 'courtesy' visit. They notified me that we – you and I – were to stop poking around in matters that don't concern us."

"They have no right to tell us what we can and can't do on board this ship," Diana announced. "We are first-class passengers and we will not be told what to do."

"The men made it very clear that if we continued snooping, they would begin breaking bones," David advised.

"And you took them seriously?" Diana sounded amazed.

"You had to have been there to appreciate the subtlety of the situation."

"That's it. We're going down to see the doctor. If you feel too threatened, you may stay up here. I'm sure I'll be fine."

She got to her feet and looked expectantly down at David. He reluctantly stood and faced her. "You realise the men said they'd beat me. They never mentioned doing you any harm."

"I should hope not!" With a flip of her hair, she turned and headed for the nearest stairwell. "And before you say anything – we will be using the ship's deck plan to find our way. This is way too important to leave to your amateur exploration antics."

David reluctantly followed her despite knowing perfectly well how to get to the infirmary by that point. At Diana's insistence, they stopped by the purser's office and obtained a map. Diana also asked the young man behind the counter the quickest way to the infirmary. He seemed hesitant to give up that information until Diana gave him her 'I'm a first-class passenger' speech. He reluctantly gave up the directions.

They ended up midship on E Deck. The infirmary was clearly signposted as being a little further down the passageway.

The door was closed when they reached the infirmary but Diana, without any thought of knocking, opened it and stepped inside. David followed. He just knew that this visit was going to lead to his meeting up with the two thugs again.

"Hello," she called out. "Hello. Is anybody here?"

There was no reply.

"Damn," she exclaimed.

"Shh." David held a finger against his lips.

"Wha…"

He shushed her again. She grudgingly stopped making noise. David pointed down the small passageway. He could hear very soft music coming from further down the narrow corridor. Diana then heard it, too. They tiptoed along until they reached the far end. The music was coming from the other side of the double doors.

David was about to knock when Diana turned the handle and opened the door.

The doctor was sitting at a small desk off to the side of the examination room. A portable record player emitted some gentle jazz music while a cigarette burned in a cut-glass ashtray sending a slow spiral of smoke into the air. A bottle of single malt Scotch sat next to it. It was only a third full. The doctor had a glass halfway to his mouth. He initially stared at the two in anger, then, upon recognising them, he shook his head in defeat and downed the contents of the glass.

"I take it my strong-arm approach didn't work?"

"What's really going on, Doctor?" Diana asked. "As passengers on board this ship we have every right to know about something that could threaten our lives."

"Yeah!" David added bravely.

"Had you said those words to me yesterday, I would have disagreed wholeheartedly. Today, however, my sentiment has changed. You may as well know what's going on. You should be given time to prepare yourselves."

"Prepare ourselves for what exactly?" Diana asked as she stepped closer to him.

"You may want to keep a few steps away." The doctor leaned over and lifted his right trouser leg. The limb was blackish green. The necrosis had consumed the entire calf and was moving up and across the doctor's knee.

Diana stumbled backwards.

"So, it is contagious?" David asked.

"We have no idea. It is certainly spreading, but we don't know how. It seems almost random."

"But I saw you with a passenger last night who also had whatever it is."

"Ah. You saw that, did you? That was the second case. Overnight there were seven more. I never came into contact with any of those other poor sods."

The doctor poured himself another drink.

"Does it hurt?" Diana asked.

"Strangely, no. Not at all. There's an odd feeling of numbness and a mild tingling, but no pain whatsoever."

"What can we do?" David asked.

"I do have one request that you may find a bit unusual. Would you mind staying here with me until it's over? From what I've observed so far, it should only take about ten to fifteen minutes more. I regret to say that I'm a tad scared of death and would feel more comfortable to not have to die here alone."

"Of course we will," Diana said. "David, why don't you see if you could find us some chairs and maybe a couple of glasses."

David gave her an understanding nod then left the room. He found a couple of folding chairs in the next room and a water cooler with a paper cup dispenser. He returned to the examination room and set up the chairs.

He poured a large Scotch for the doctor and two smaller ones in disposable paper cups for himself and Diana.

As they settled in their chairs, the doctor spoke.

"This was to be my last crossing. My wife, Vera, and I were going to buy a small cottage in Felpham, in West Sussex. It's a small village just down the coast from Bognor Regis. It's a lovely spot right on the sea. We've been planning it for over thirty years. For all those years I've been away at sea far more than I've been by her side. We both understood that that was my life and did the best we could to accept it and live with the separation. I always knew how lonely she felt each time I set sail but we knew the time would come when we would be together every day. Now that we're within spitting distance of that dream, I'm apparently not going to make it home after all."

"I'm so sorry, Doctor." Diana looked close to tears.

"My name's William. There's little point in using formal titles now. I'll be before Saint Peter soon enough, and I doubt he'd be impressed with them either."

"Is there anything we can do for you?" David offered.

"It would have been nice to let Vera know, but that's sadly not in the cards, either."

"We could send her a wire pretending it's from you, or tell her what's actually happened. Whichever you prefer," Diana said.

"That would be very nice except there's no way of communicating with the shore," William advised.

"Of course there is. The ship has a wireless telephone and telegraph. I know that for a fact. My father uses it quite often."

"It does indeed, miss. Unfortunately, it's not been working for a few days. It stopped at the same time as the bridge..."

The doctor shivered and bowed his head.

"I don't think there's long for me now."

"What were you saying about the bridge?" David prodded.

Diana slapped his arm. She clearly didn't feel it was the right time to cross-examine a dying man.

The doctor tried to sit up straight. They could see the necrosis rising above his shirt collar. It slowly climbed his neck then inched up over his jaw. As with the passenger David had observed the previous night, his jaw suddenly dropped open as the tendons and ligatures eroded to mush.

The doctor tried to speak.

"I'm so sorr..." His mouth was consumed before he could finish.

David reached over and took Diana's hand as they watched William's last moments. The necrosis was just below his eyes. For a moment they could see the sparkle of life within them, then they turned opaque, blackened, then began to prune.

Diana looked away as the crud reached his forehead. As it encircled the top of his head, David gave her a nudge.

"I think you should see this part."

She reluctantly turned back and they both watched as all the exposed parts of him began to shimmer at the edges. Minute wisps of green matter spun off him, then disappeared. The wisps were replaced with a powdery green aura as his entire body was consumed by death. Then, in a split second, his mortal remains vanished as did the green haze. His clothes collapsed onto the chair and floor, flatter, yet almost in the shape they had held when occupied.

David turned to Diana. Her eyes were riveted to the doctor's chair. The only sound in the room was the portable record player as it dropped another album onto the turntable. The arm swung over to the vinyl's edge and the needle lowered into the first groove. There was a hiss while it searched for the recorded sound.

A slow blues ballad played. The singer was a soulful black woman. Her voice filled the room.

'What am I supposed to do, now that you be gone? You promised I would be your woman, but you done left me all alone.

You was meant to fill my life with love, and tenderness.

But all I'm left with now is sorrow and an unused wedding dress.'

Eventually, Diana and David made their way topside and stood at a railing on Sun Deck, staring out into the swirling fog. They looked down the black hull but couldn't see the waterline.

They remained silent, trapped in their own thoughts. Diana slipped an arm through David's.

"May I ask you a big favour?"

"Of course. Anything," he answered.

"Without any questions or inhibitions or commitments – would you please take me to bed?"

He turned and looked questioningly into her eyes.

"That was one of the most profoundly sad things I've

ever seen in my life," Diana whispered. "I suddenly need to feel very alive and very loved. Does that make sense?"

"Yes. I feel the same way," David replied. "Why don't I go down ahead, then you follow in a few minutes. Hopefully, nobody will see us."

"No. Enough of this clandestine nonsense!" Diana took his hand in hers and together they headed down to Main Deck.

CHAPTER
TEN

They spent the rest of the day in each other's arms. Their moods rose and fell with their passions. There was a desperation within them both. They were aware only of fulfilling their own needs as daylight hours passed and the outside world donned its nightly cloak of darkness.

At some point, Diana left the rumpled bed and slipped out of the cabin. When David woke, it was just past 8 p.m. A note was leant against the bedside table lamp.

It simply read 'You're lovely.' David realised that he was starving and that he needed to be around people for a while. He considered having a bath, but wanted Diana's scent to linger on him for as long as possible.

He had never in his life felt such an overwhelming sense of emotional perfection as when their bodies became one. When they had made love, they were no longer bound by any physical realities. They seemed almost to have crossed into a dimension filled with nothing but their own heightened sensations.

David realised that for the first time in many years, he was feeling happy.

The thought terrified him.

Along with the feeling of joy was the realisation that he was obviously no longer destined to take his own life. Diana had stolen that selfish plan and rendered it utterly obsolete.

He sat on the edge of his bed and quietly sobbed. Different emotions battled inside him. He felt a sense of peace that he'd never thought attainable. He also felt an indescribable relief at not having to curtail his lifespan. He couldn't even imagine how he'd ever considered something so drastic. Why hadn't he realised that he had everything to live for? He tried to convince himself that such feelings were not predicated solely on Diana being part of his life. But he now knew that they very much were.

David got dressed and walked aft to the Veranda Grill. He was advised that there would be a short wait for a table to open up, so he sat at the bar and ordered a large Manhattan on the rocks.

He turned to face the room and was surprised at how normal everything looked. Elegant people were enjoying themselves while dining in the restaurant's lavish surroundings. The women had all dressed specially for the occasion. The men wore their best suits and ties.

None of the passengers seemed even remotely aware that people were dying on the *Oceanis*. Three people were dead so far, and those were just the ones that David had witnessed. The doctor mentioned seven others. It seemed that no one had a clue as to the real number. He wondered at what point the captain would declare an onboard emergency? Would he call for a curfew, or worse, a complete quarantine with passengers forced to remain locked in their cabins?

As he looked around the room, he couldn't imagine that anything could break the spell of that evening.

He didn't need to imagine it.

Reality took care of that in the form of the ship's first officer. He was in his mid-forties and looked extremely fit. His black hair was just starting to turn grey at the temples. He had Royal Navy written all over him. The formal dress whites were almost redundant. He entered the grill and spoke in a hushed tone with the maître d'. A finger was then pointed directly at David.

The officer approached him and held out a hand. "Mr Easton, sir. I am Commander Isaac Hess. The captain requests your company in his quarters."

David shook the offered hand. "I was about to have something to eat."

"The captain has arranged a small buffet. I believe you will find it more than adequate."

David wasn't fully convinced. He had visions of being tricked into the engine compartment where the two thugs from earlier would be waiting to carry out their previous threat.

"Shall we?" The officer gestured for David to join him.

"If we make one move towards engineering, the deal's off," David announced.

"I beg your pardon, sir?" Commander Hess had no idea what David was on about.

Hess led David out of the cocktail lounge and into the same staircase lobby he'd passed through earlier, but instead of heading down, the first officer climbed another flight then emerged on the aft end of the sun deck. They walked past the two deck housings beneath the giant funnels. David couldn't see their tops due to the fog. It seemed to be sitting even lower that night.

They reached an external staircase that led to a narrow, wood-panelled passageway. David could see that it ended at the ship's bridge. He felt privileged to be allowed into such a vital part of the ship.

Just before the bridge there was a plain wood-panelled door on the right with a discreet brass notice that simply read 'Captain'. Hess gave the door two sharp knocks.

"Enter," the captain's voice boomed from the other side of the door. Hess opened it for David to enter, then closed it gently with himself on the outside.

David was surprised to find himself in a small, cosy sitting room, complete with a coal fireplace against one wall. Two floral-print sofas sat facing each other on either side of the hearth.

What looked to be an authentic Queen Anne-period dining table and chairs sat at the far end of the room. A selection of hors d'oeuvres, breads and cheeses sat between opened bottles of red and white wine.

What surprised David the most was that Diana and her father were sitting on one of the sofas, plates in hand. David felt as if he was disturbing a private cocktail party.

Captain Havelin stepped forward and vigorously shook his hand. "Nice you could join us, Mr Easton."

David could see that the captain was looking older. Though the man had to be in his late sixties, he still carried himself like a younger man. His full head of white hair was thinning and his face showed the lines of a well-lived life. David couldn't help but notice the dark circles under the older man's eyes. Clearly events had been keeping him awake at night.

"Please accept my apologies for the suddenness of this little get-together," Havelin said. "Help yourself to a glass of wine or we have sherry if you'd prefer. There are some finger foods on the table as well."

Once David had given himself a decent selection of nibbles and had poured himself a glass of Bâtard-Montrachet, he sat across from the Olsons.

Captain Havelin remained standing. "It has come to my attention that some of you – Mr Easton, certainly – have become aware of a slight problem that has manifested itself on board the *Oceanis*."

"Isn't the term '*slight problem*', somewhat of an understatement?" Diana asked.

The captain gave her a long, studying look. It was doubtful that in his lengthy naval career, too many people had questioned his words without rebuke. To have such a thing occur at the hands of a woman seemed to be entirely foreign to him.

"Quite." He forced a smile for her benefit. "As you are aware, we have tragically lost a number of souls to what some of the officers are referring to as the green plague. I should first point out that it is not a plague as we understand the term. It is something completely different. Something neither myself nor the ship's doctor have ever seen before. Actually, I was hoping that the good doctor would join us tonight but he seems to have been detained."

"He hasn't been detained. He's dead," David advised.

The captain visibly paled and had to sit. "I had no idea."

"David and I were with him when he passed," Diana said. "It happened earlier today."

"So, you've seen it? You've seen what happens in the final moments?"

"Yes. We both have," David replied.

"It was strangely peaceful," Diana added.

"I have so far not witnessed this – what should we call it? A wasting disease? But my daughter has explained the final stages in vivid detail," Arthur said. "I feel that this shouldn't be something that's kept from the passengers. People are dying from a disease that is consuming their bodies in a matter of minutes. They need to be aware so that they might take precautions."

The captain studied Arthur for a moment.

"If this were made public, there would be ship-wide panic. There is no benefit in alerting everyone on board, at least until we know more about it. At present, we can't stop it or treat it because we don't know what it is or what's causing it. The infections seem random, yet to date it has affected all classes of passenger, officers and the crew. One member of a family may contract it yet the other members are left unaffected. There also appears to be no symptoms of the green plague until the effects of the necrosis have begun. When we had the first case with your steward Andrew, it took over four hours from the first indication of the malady to his being fully consumed."

"So, you don't think it's contagious?" Arthur asked.

"Actually, no. I don't," the captain said. "There have been twenty-seven suspected deaths…"

"Suspected?" Diana interrupted.

"As you yourself have witnessed, no trace of the physical body remains after the necrosis runs its course. We have no way of knowing if that number is accurate or not. People tend to – how can I put this? There is a tendency for some passengers to cabin hop when on board ship. Some of the missing may just have found alternate entertainment in other people's cabins. By the same token, people may have passed quietly in their own cabins and we would never know. The entire situation is a complete conundrum."

"Don't you think it's time you tried to find out the actual number of deaths so far?" Arthur asked. "A cabin check would give you and your crew a much better idea of the accurate count."

"It would indeed, Mr Olson. It would also doubtless lead to ship-wide panic. At that point, there would be no restraint. There would be no order. Just a level of chaos that I cannot permit on my ship. Besides, checking a cabin to see if people aren't there, is illogical."

"There would be some trace, wouldn't there?" David pointed out.

"Would there? Clothes left on the floor are not an uncommon sight in a ship's cabin. You would be surprised just how messy some people can be."

"What about a roll call? You could do another lifeboat drill as was done upon departure. Then your crew could check everyone's names at their boat station," Diana suggested.

"Despite the mandatory nature of the lifeboat drill, attendance is not guaranteed. We estimate that at best we get eighty-five per cent turnout. The first-class passengers are by far the worst offenders for not showing up."

"There must be…" David tried to speak.

The captain talked over him. "There is another facet to this tragedy of which you are not as yet aware. A facet that makes secrecy even more essential." The captain looked to the other three, wondering how to phrase the next statement.

"I presume that you have all noticed that we have been enshrouded in a deep fog for some time?"

The three nodded their agreement.

"What you haven't been aware of is that, though we have been making way at cruising speed, there is no indication that the ship has actually moved at all. The instruments have all held the same position since the fog first arrived."

"Have you taken a sextant reading?" Arthur asked.

Captain Havelin smiled at him. "We have not, sir. We need clear skies to take a celestial reading. Even a slight break in the cloud would suffice but this fog has not broken for a second."

"I assume you have contacted either New York or Southampton. What do they have to say?" Arthur was clearly growing impatient.

"We have not spoken to the shore or to any other vessels since the fog first enveloped us."

"I understand you're not wishing to cause a panic but to intentionally not notify the authorities on shore is putting the entire ship in danger!" Arthur boomed.

"I didn't say we haven't tried to contact those on shore or any vessels in our proximity. The fact is, we have been trying nonstop. All of our equipment seems to be working perfectly, yet whatever we try, ship to shore telephony, long and medium-range radio, even wireless telegraphy – we receive no confirmation back."

"But I've been sending wires every day," Arthur insisted.

"You have indeed, sir. However, we don't know whether any of them have been received since this condition began. We think that something within the fog bank is shielding us and not letting any signals leave the ship."

"That's impossible," Diana stated. "Isn't it?"

"There must be something you can do," David said. "Have you tried steering the ship in a circle or some direction other than the current heading?"

"Yes, we have. Multiple times, in fact."

"And what happened?" Diana asked.

"We don't know," the captain replied. "The instruments stay locked to the same point. They show no movement or directional change."

The captain studied the group.

"You now have a better understanding of why we can't let the other passengers know about this. We hope that this fog will finally lift, but until then, we need to carry on as if all is normal aboard ship."

"Captain," Arthur said, "why have you chosen to share this information with us?"

"Basically, because your daughter and Mr Easton have already become aware of there being something amiss regarding the steward. What I didn't know was that you both had also witnessed the green plague. I felt it best to share the specifics of the wider situation with you all so that you might be persuaded to stop your amateur investigating. I would prefer you to be part of my inner circle rather than stumbling around the ship, asking random questions and potentially causing panic."

"Captain, has anyone tried to lower a lifeboat to check if it can move away from the ship and maybe see how deep the fog bank really is?" Diana asked.

The captain looked impressed. "That was one of our first thoughts, but we are not able to lower any of the boats at the moment."

"For God's sake, why?" Arthur asked.

"The lifeboat davits appear to be rusted solid."

"That's a disgrace. When were they last serviced?"

"As per US regulations, they were serviced prior to this voyage and were inspected by a US Coastguard official," the captain replied with just a trace of disdain.

"Are you telling us that they rusted to the point of disrepair in a matter of days?" Arthur kept on at him.

"Regretfully I am. May I suggest that we take a stroll down to Sun Deck so that you may all have a look for yourselves?"

David glugged the last of his glass of wine then joined the others as they left the captain's cabin and made their way down the crew-only exterior stairway.

"May I request that you do not draw attention to the lifeboats or the rust. As far as the other passengers are concerned, I am simply explaining to you how the lifeboats are meant to function in the event of an emergency."

The others agreed.

The captain led them to the first boat on the starboard side. He gestured to the curved davit arm that supported one end of the emergency craft. He explained that, in the event of there being a need to lower a lifeboat, the davit operator would swing it out over the sea and away from the ship then via a pulley system, lower the boat to the water.

"Please take special note of the mechanism at the base of the davit arm," he advised.

The three leaned over and could clearly see that what had once been a large and functional brass hinge mechanism was now covered in a green casing which had lines of red rust that seemed to have dripped down the side of the fitting.

The three took care to not act surprised or shocked.

"Are they all like that?" Diana whispered.

"For the most part, yes. Some, like this lifeboat, have a few other anomalies," the captain advised.

"Such as what?" Arthur asked with growing concern.

"Miss Olson, you appear to be the smallest and fittest one among us. Would you be so kind as to dip under the lifeboat and then lean against the railing and face back so that you'll be looking at the outfacing side of the craft."

Without a moment's hesitation, she checked to see if anyone was looking, then did exactly as the captain had suggested. It was dark, but there was just enough ambient light reflected back off the fog for her to make out the offside of the lifeboat. She couldn't work out what she was seeing. It looked to be a very solid, brightly painted craft but something was wrong. The painted hull should have been smooth yet what she was looking at was uneven and looked to have hairline cracks all over the hull. She reached up and felt the boat's exterior.

She gasped.

She dipped under the lifeboat and re-joined the group. She stared blankly at the captain. He simply raised his eyebrows in understanding.

"What did you see?" David asked.

She held out her hand. In it was a greenish mush with streaks of white paint crusted upon it. "It's almost completely rotten. That entire side of the lifeboat is – like this."

She closed her hand and squeezed the mush. Greenish ooze ran down her fingers and splattered onto the deck.

"Are they all like that?" she asked.

"No. Only a few have deteriorated to this degree."

"But only on the outside? So, no one on board can see it?" Her voice sounded almost hollow.

"What could possibly cause something like that?" her father asked.

"I regret to say that we have no idea whatsoever. We believe it may have something to do with the fog. It may have some chemical property that reacts with metal and wood, and is eating away at the ship's outer edge."

"So, are we to understand that at this time there are no working lifeboats on board the *Oceanis*? What if we were to take on water; there would be no way to abandon ship?" Arthur asked.

"I regret to say that that is indeed the current situation," Havelin acknowledged. "Whatever that fog is, it appears to be crippling the ship."

"There's another option," David said. "What if everything beyond the fog has been destroyed and the fog is the only thing protecting us from what's out there?"

"That's impossible," Diana said.

"Is it?" David turned to her. "We are on an ocean liner that isn't moving, has no communications, is trapped in a fog bank and people are turning to dust. It seems to me that the impossible has now become our reality."

The four slowly turned and faced out into the dense, swirling grey fog. The lights from the ship seemed to highlight individual whirls and eddies.

It almost seemed alive.

CHAPTER
ELEVEN

The group disbanded without another word being said. Arthur returned to his suite while Diana and David went back to his cabin. Lovemaking wasn't even remotely on their minds. They needed to talk and it had to be somewhere private.

"Why didn't your mother come along?" David asked.

"My father felt that you and her together in the same room would undoubtedly derail the whole tenet of the conversation."

"You mean I'm still not on her Christmas card list?" David joked.

"Don't hold your breath for that," she replied. "She's a stubborn woman."

"Why do you think the captain invited you and your father to meet with him? You and I are supposed to be the troublemakers."

"He didn't invite us. We invited the captain. My father

got word to him that we wanted to speak with him before panic broke out."

"Why wasn't I initially invited?" David asked.

"I told my father about the two goons that came to your cabin. He wanted to make sure that there was no chance of a repeat incident," Diana explained. "Once we had the captain's word that threats of violence were off the table as far as you were concerned, they sent for you to join us."

"I guess I should thank you," David said.

"Actually, you should thank my father. This was all his idea. He's taken a liking to you. I can't imagine why." She suppressed a grin.

"Probably because of our little tête-à-tête the other night. He seemed very..." David suddenly looked crestfallen.

"What's wrong?" she asked.

"The wires he sent about me to New York; if what the captain said was true, they never got there, did they?" he sighed.

"I wouldn't worry. If we survive this, I am sure he'll make certain that your situation is reversed as he promised."

"I take it he told you everything we discussed that night?"

"Right up to and including his request for you to not force your nudity on my mother."

"Talk about things that should never have to be said out loud," David grinned.

"So, what is your plan, Mr Easton?"

"With us, or the situation on board?" he asked.

"I somehow think that those are unfortunately very closely intertwined. If we can't stop the green plague, there won't be any us, will there?" she stated.

"That was bluntly put."

Diana shrugged her shoulders.

"Do you have any ideas?" David asked.

"Ladies' room first. May I?" She gestured to the bathroom.

"Of course."

Diana opened the door and turned on the lights.

"Oh shit." She backed away from the door. She looked terrified.

"Don't be so theatrical. I know I left it in a bit of a mess earlier, but really." He joined her at the bathroom door and looked into the room.

"Oh shit!"

The pristine tiled walls, the white enamelled bathroom suite and the luxuriously fluffy towels were gone. As were the lights. The bathroom looked like a mouldy cave. The walls were covered in a thick greyish-green ooze. Barnacles and ocean vegetation were everywhere. Sea grass was slowly wafting back and forth as if being governed by some invisible tidal flow. The ceiling was no longer there. Instead, a few rusted metal beams were all they could see.

The sparkling stainless-steel taps and faucets were nothing more than rusted nubs. They looked to be suffering from the same degenerative force as the lifeboat hinges.

Then there was the odour. The room smelled of long-term decay and rot. It was cloying. It smelled like death.

As they watched in stupefied horror, a pale, almost translucent starfish moved into view at the bottom of the slime-coated bathtub.

David was about to speak when the room started to shimmer, then as if in a movie dissolve, it began to morph back into its normal self. As they watched in utter amazement, the pristine bathroom returned. David's wet towel was back on the floor. His toothbrush was back in its precarious position on the edge of the sink. Even the smell had gone, though there was the slightest trace of a mouldy odour coming from somewhere.

They both leaned in and had a quick look, but neither seemed to have the urge to step any further into the room.

"Looks safe now, if you still need to use it?" David advised.

"I may never pee again," she replied weakly.

"That could be painful," he tried to joke. "I think we need air."

They exited the stairway lobby on Sun Deck. It was one in the morning so they had the place to themselves. At least they thought they did. Once past the first funnel deck housing they heard voices coming from the other side of the ship.

It sounded like a bunch of young people having fun. After the dour meeting with the captain, then the incident in the cabin, sounds of frivolity seemed almost otherworldly.

They made their way around funnel number two, hoping that some of the laughter would rub off on them. As they rounded the corner they saw a group of about twenty kids, all in their teens, having a whale of a time.

The girls were laughing almost uncontrollably as the men showed off.

It took a few moments for Diana and David to fully grasp what it was that they were seeing.

The teens had built a ramp from deckchairs, cushions and folding tables. It sloped from the deck up to the edge of the railing. About ten feet further aft, a dozen deckchair cushions were placed side by side, forming a giant mattress.

They watched as a young man in slacks and a dress shirt ran barefoot, full tilt, up the wobbly ramp, then threw himself off the side of the ship and into the fog. He screamed in delight as he vanished from view within the grey mass.

Not more than ten seconds later he shot back out of the fog, sailed over the railing and landed on the deckchair cushions with a celebratory hoot. He got to his feet and bowed for the ladies.

The onlookers went crazy. Their actions seemed almost tribal. There was no restraint. Just euphoric joy.

The next one up the ramp was a young girl who hardly seemed old enough to be part of the group. She looked to be no more than twelve or thirteen. She wore a delicate pink formal dress. Her feet were also bare. She ran up the ramp with a look of intense determination.

She made it to the top and like the person before her, vaulted into the air and into the fog. The others started chanting her name.

"Mary!"

"Mary!"

"Mary!"

It took longer for her to reappear. After almost twenty seconds she flew back out of the greyness and landed on the cushions.

She got up a little unsteadily, then fist-punched the sky.

David and Diana couldn't help but notice that her evening dress was torn in a number of places. Mary also appeared to have a line of green slime on one leg going from above her hem line, to her ankle.

She didn't appear to care.

The next person at the ramp seemed to be having trouble. His steps were uncertain and unsteady.

Diana and David assumed the cause was too much alcohol.

"Come on, Peter. You can do it," someone shouted.

Peter suddenly took off his shirt. The crowd cheered.

Diana threw a hand to her mouth.

The greenish-black necrosis was already at his shoulders and was climbing quickly.

The others didn't seem at all phased. They continued to cheer him on.

Peter couldn't make it up the ramp.

A dozen people grabbed him and carried him to the railing. The necrosis had reached his face. They swung him back and forth like a pendulum until they had enough momentum to hurl him overboard and into the fog.

They all stood watching in silence. Nothing happened for over two minutes, then something soared back out of the grey and rolled onto the mattress. One of the onlookers grabbed it. It unfurled. It was Peter's trousers wrapped around his brown dress shoes.

They all cheered hysterically.

Then they noticed David and Diana.

The teens all slowly turned and stared at the couple. Their eyes seemed to glow. Diana and David knew it was just a reflection from the deck lighting, but the effect was still unnerving. They looked possessed.

They continued to stare, without sound or movement, until one of them broke the spell and shouted, "My turn!" He then started running up the makeshift ramp as the others turned away from David and Diana and focused on their freakish new way of having fun.

David took Diana's hand and cautiously walked them out of view behind the funnel deck housing.

"I really hope we don't see that becoming a formal activity listed in the *Daily Log*," David tried to joke.

Diana looked deeply into his eyes.

"What's going on, David?"

CHAPTER
TWELVE

David woke to find Diana snuggled up next to him. She was sound asleep. Her head was resting on his shoulder. He tried to gently move her, but with no success. She was out for the count. He tried sliding his arm out from under her, but found it was completely numb.

He suddenly and irrationally felt trapped. He took a couple of deep breaths to try and calm himself.

"What on earth are you doing?" she asked, her voice still thick with sleep.

"Trying to free my arm. It's gone to sleep."

"Lucky arm." She rolled to the side, enabling him to slide it out from under her. It wasn't that easy. It was numb and only mildly responsive. His hand was completely useless.

He managed to free himself and sit up. He held his sleeping arm with his working hand and tried to shake it back to life.

"Ouch!"

"What now?" Diana asked.

"Pins and needles!" he replied.

"I really need you to be my hero at the moment but every so often you reveal a very disturbing wimpy side."

"Actually, most of me is wimpy. You just occasionally manage to see a smidge of manliness."

She smiled as she sat up next to him. "I wonder what fresh hell today will bring?"

"Well, we've already got plague and pestilence, if my bathroom was anything to go by, so, I think we're about due for the rain of frogs."

"Actual frogs or French people?" she joked. "I always get that confused."

He tried to force a smile. "I can't stop thinking about those kids last night. What were they doing?"

"We saw what they were doing. The question is, how did they first think to actually try it? Throwing yourself overboard into a dense fog isn't something that suddenly dawns on you. You're not going to suddenly sit up and think, 'I know, let's jump off the ship and see if the friendly cloud throws us back.'"

"They did," David said.

"Did you notice how they weren't the least bit fazed by that guy with the plague? They were all perfectly happy to touch him."

"And throw him off the ship. Let's not forget that part," he reminded her.

She gave him a concerned look.

"They also didn't seem surprised when he didn't come back."

"He couldn't come back. He would have completely disintegrated by then."

"We knew that because we saw it first-hand. How the hell did they know? I mean, they all seemed to know a lot more about the fog than we do – didn't they?" she asked.

"That whole thing was so surreal. I just hope it was a one-off. Those kids had all the makings of some sort of a mob. That's the last thing we need," David added.

"They were just having fun," Diana suggested.

"Going to the movies is fun. Playing tennis is fun. Throwing yourself and others off the side of an ocean liner in the middle of the Atlantic is psychotic," David countered.

"I can't argue with that," Diana said. "I just wish I knew – why them? Why a bunch of kids?"

"Maybe it's all about their youth. What if there's a stage before the necrosis starts, when younger people start behaving oddly? Perhaps in older people there's a switch that doesn't get thrown."

"Maybe it has to do with puberty. They all seemed to be the right age," Diana suggested.

"Who knows? I'm not exactly sure what that insight gives us, anyway," David remarked.

"We've been so intrigued with why those kids were doing what they were doing that we forgot one major thing," she said.

"Go on. Amaze me," David said.

"The fog was actually throwing the kids back onto the boat," she pointed out. "I've been around a lot of fog in New York and I honestly can't remember that being one of its abilities."

"You're right. That is by far the weirdest part," David stated. "I joked last night about it being alive. Maybe it wasn't a joke. Is that even possible?"

"Not as we understand the current definition of alive," Diana replied.

"But when you consider what the captain was telling us, plus what we saw those kids doing, it does kind of seem like it doesn't want the ship or anything on it leaving this position."

"Instead of jumping to the supernatural, shouldn't we fully dismiss the probable?" Diana suggested.

"Kind of like Occam's razor?"

"The simplest solution is most likely the right one," Diana paraphrased the famous principle.

"Wow. I'm impressed," David voiced.

"Because a woman knows something clever?"

"No. I'm impressed that anyone knows about Occam's principle. It's not exactly common knowledge outside the scientific community."

"I do read. Remember?" She rolled her eyes.

"I will endeavour to never praise you again – ever," he joked.

David got to his feet and opened the curtains covering the portholes. He stared at them with a new sense of foreboding. Diana sensed his mood change and joined him.

"What is that?"

"I haven't a clue, but I don't think it's a good thing," David said as he closely inspected one of the ports. The outside of the glass had turned dark green as if someone had painted the safety glass during the night. That would have been troubling enough, but the polished brass port surrounds and hinges were no longer gleaming and did not look remotely functional. They had turned a mottled black and were oozing rust down the varnished wood wall covering. Where the rust dribbles met the carpet, there was a growing red stain.

David felt it. It was wet.

"Should we try to open it?" Diana asked.

"I personally think that whatever seems to be happening out there, should stay out there. Don't you?"

"Well, should we at least tell someone?" Diana suggested.

David was about to make a sarcastic comment, then decided she had a point. He stepped over to the internal phone and dialled zero. The phone rang for an unusually long time before a harried-sounding operator answered. David advised her that something seemed to be wrong with their portholes and asked if she could get someone from maintenance to stop by.

"I'll try and have someone come to your cabin as soon as possible, but we seem to be having a great number of issues with passenger cabins this morning."

David asked if they needed to wait for the maintenance person. He was informed that she couldn't give a specific time but that engineering had passkeys.

"I think we should get out of here and get some breakfast. I have a feeling we're going to need to keep our energy levels up." David then had a thought. "Do you need to go back to your parents' suite?"

"Probably. At some point. Even if it's just to pick up a few things," she said.

"Are you planning on moving in?" he grinned.

"Not if you don't keep your cabin better maintained. It's a disgrace," she quipped.

As they left, David noticed that there was no *Daily Log*. For some reason, he found that the paper's absence was more frightening than almost anything else that had happened. It was an indicator of just how badly things were starting to fall apart.

The main dining room was not as full as usual. Each table seemed to be missing one or two people. Those who were present were talking in hushed tones. The passengers were obviously starting to notice that something was wrong. David wondered if they had woken to find rusted portholes or slime-filled bathrooms. He couldn't imagine that that pleasure had solely been reserved for him and Diana.

Neither of them had much of an appetite after the bathroom then porthole incidents. They ended up having cereal just to get something into their stomachs. Diana was having trouble even with cold cornflakes.

"You know – I probably should check in on my parents. It's one thing to rebel against my mother, it's something else entirely to ignore her, especially while all this is going on."

"I couldn't agree more. Do you want me to come with you?" David asked.

"I want to make sure she's all right, not give her a heart attack."

"Funny, the effect I have on women," David replied.

"Hilarious!" She glared at him. "What will you do while I'm gone?"

"I want to try an experiment with the fog," he said.

"If you're thinking of jumping overboard – I would like to remind you that we decided that was absolutely not going to happen. Certainly not so long as I'm around."

"No. No jumping overboard. I plan on sending other objects into the fog." He gave her a serious stare as he unobtrusively pocketed the table's salt and pepper shakers as well as a handful of bread rolls from the centre of the table.

"Please don't get caught," she whispered.

"They're hardly likely to put me in the brig for this," he reassured her.

"I'm sure you're right. I just don't want to be seen as the sad spinster who had to settle for a halfwit that liked to steal things from breakfast tables so he could throw them overboard."

"Point well taken," he replied. "I'll be discreet."

Diana rolled her eyes as she stood. "Where should we meet?"

"How about the main lounge in about an hour?" he suggested. "Wish me luck."

David could see the dread in her eyes. He watched her leave the dining room. He had one last gulp of his coffee, then headed to the grand staircase. He reached Sun Deck, then casually walked to a sheltered deck area close to the railing. He intentionally didn't want to use the same spot as the teens had done the night before. For his experiment, he needed a completely different location.

He wasn't sure what the results would actually prove but he felt it had to be done. Knowledge was, after all, power. The problem was that David didn't know whether having the knowledge but not understanding it still counted or not.

He looked out into the fog for a good few minutes before retrieving the silver-plated salt shaker from his pocket. He quickly looked to see that he was still alone, then threw it hard into the greyness. It immediately vanished from sight. David waited but nothing happened. He stood there for a full minute, then pulled the pepper shaker from his other pocket. He threw that into the fog in approximately the same place.

Still nothing happened.

Disappointed, David then threw his two bread rolls, one at a time. After a further two minutes during which none of the objects returned, he turned away from the fog intending to return below deck. He stopped in his tracks. Captain Havelin was standing less than ten feet from him. He was smiling knowingly back at him.

"It takes longer with inanimate objects. Wait about another sixty seconds," Havelin advised.

David glanced from the captain to the fog, then back to the captain.

"Looks to me like nothing's going to…"

The salt and pepper shakers flew back out of the fog only seconds apart and hit the exterior of the deck housing where the ship's kennels were located. David cautiously picked them up and saw that they were both heavily tarnished and corroded. A moment later, the bread rolls flew out of the mist and landed on the deck with a wet, squelching sound. David didn't pick those up. They were covered in a furry grey-green mould.

"Is that what you were hoping to discover?" the captain asked.

"I'm not sure what I was hoping for. I just wanted to see if lifeless objects interacted the same way with the fog."

"You've doubtless encountered some of our younger passengers engaging in their new pastime?" Havelin asked.

"We saw them last night," David replied.

"There were a few groups dotted around the ship. We finally had to ask them to disband."

"And did they?"

"Actually, they did. They even dismantled their ramps and put everything back where they'd found it."

"Bizarre," David commented.

"So, what have you learned from throwing condiments and food off the ship?" Havelin asked with a trace of sarcasm.

"Not much. Only that nothing seems to be able to leave the *Oceanis*. I was hoping to be able to come up with something a little less mundane as far as a premise for the whole thing."

"I know the feeling," the captain replied. "We did the same experiment a few days ago. It's as if the fog doesn't want the ship to get rid of anything. It wants everything in its original place."

"What could that possibly mean?" David asked.

"Unfortunately, we don't know. It's just a useless observation. Unfortunately, we have no shortage of those at the present time." He took a moment to ponder something. "Have you or Miss Olson seen anything that you would consider unusual? Other than the boomerang effect of the fog."

"You know we have. We were with the doct…"

"Not the deaths. I was meaning things like – visions or hallucinations. Have you seen parts of the ship appear to be in a different condition than normal?" The captain tried to be as tactful as possible.

"If you mean, did we see my cabin bathroom turn into a mouldy tomb, then yes. We saw that earlier today."

"Did it return to normal?" Captain Havelin asked.

"Yes, it did, though I'm not sure I want to go in there anymore," David advised.

The captain nodded his head gravely. "People throughout the ship have seen similar things. This morning, I saw the bridge as little more than an empty shell covered in sea growth and rust. All the safety glass was gone. Then a moment later it returned to normal."

"Hopefully, unlike my bathroom, you still plan to continue using the bridge for its intended purpose."

Havelin smiled. "Indeed, we shall, at least once the bridge resumes having a purpose."

"So, no one has any idea what's happening? Why we're seeing things? Why the fog is doing what it's doing?" David tried to keep his voice calm.

"Among the officers there's one theory that seems to make sense. That is, if one can consider the absurd to be remotely sensible. They think that the cloud is causing some form of shipboard hysteria – including the hallucinations."

"That doesn't explain the green plague though, does it?" David pointed out.

"No, Mr Easton. It most certainly does not."

"So, what are we supposed to do? Just wait around for the next new and exciting oddity?"

"What we must do, Mr Easton, is stay calm," Havelin stated. "I find it doubtful that there will be any new aspects to these mysterious manifestations. Level heads will prevail and will most certainly get us through this situation."

"God, I hope you're right," David shot back.

"So do I, Mr Easton." The captain offered him an encouraging smile.

David had been sitting in the lounge for over an hour and Diana still hadn't shown up. He was starting to get concerned when he saw her father approaching from the far side of the room. He looked pale and badly shaken.

"Diana asked me to come and see if you'd mind joining us in our suite?"

"Is she all right?" David asked.

"She's perfectly fine. I'd prefer not to say anything else until we're out of public earshot," Arthur whispered.

"What about you? You don't look well."

"Let's talk below," he replied.

Not another word was spoken until they reached the door of their suite tucked away on Sun Deck, right below the bridge. Arthur held the door open for him to enter.

David was stunned. It was one of the most lavish suites he'd ever seen. It looked as if it had been transplanted from Park Avenue except for the row of oblong windows that faced the bow of the ship.

The other thing he noticed was Diana crying gently on one of the sofas as she clung to a piece of expensive-looking silk.

He kneeled in front of her. "What's happened? Are you hurt?"

She met his gaze then held out the material for him to see. He couldn't immediately grasp what she was doing, until he noticed an expensive belt and matching shoes bundled together on the floor right next to Diana.

"No!" he exclaimed. "When did it happen?"

"About fifteen minutes ago. We were talking about you, strangely enough, when she went pale and said her feet felt funny. She kicked off her shoes, and – you've seen what happens."

"Was she in any pain?" David asked.

"She didn't seem to be. In fact, she seemed suddenly quite serene." Diana started to cry harder. "I couldn't look at her face at the end. I didn't want to remember her that way. She said she loved me and I couldn't even look at her."

Arthur sat next to her. "She went very peacefully, sweetheart. You couldn't ask for more than that."

"I could ask for her not to have died at all." Diana got to her feet and gently placed her mother's dress on the sofa.

"Shit!" she screamed. "What the hell is happening? This can't be real."

David didn't know what to say. Especially after his conversation with the captain. Then there was the fact that he could see that behind Diana and Arthur, the suite's glass ports were starting to turn opaque with just a slight tinge of green. As he watched, the brass fittings began to darken and crack.

Diana looked into his eyes, searching for some hope.

He wasn't sure there was any left to give.

The captain chose that moment to make a ship-wide announcement through the vessel's emergency communication system.

"*Ladies and gentlemen, this is your captain speaking.*" His voice sounded tinny coming out of the small ceiling speakers. "*Most of you are now aware that there appears to be a shipboard malady that has affected some passengers and crew. So far, there is no definitive evidence showing it to be contagious. People throughout the ship have become infected, but in some cases, the patient has had zero contact with any other infected persons. In some people, mild hallucinations have been the only symptom. Unfortunately, in others, symptoms have been more severe. Myself and my crew are doing everything we can to hasten our arrival in port where highly trained medical professionals will take charge of treatment for those who may have contracted the illness. In the meantime, please don't panic. The best thing you can do for yourselves and for the other passengers' well-being, is to carry on with your onboard activities and continue to avail yourselves of all the fabulous amenities about the Oceanis. Thank you.*"

There was an electronic crackle, followed by complete silence.

CHAPTER
THIRTEEN

"What do you make of that?" Arthur asked the others.

"The words 'too little, too late' spring to mind," Diana voiced.

"I don't think that's going to pacify the passengers for very long," David said. "Things are deteriorating too fast. A generic verbal placation is not enough at this point."

"What else could he have said or even done?" Arthur asked. "He has to balance keeping people informed with not causing an outright panic."

"I for one feel he…"

The suite's phone chirped. Diana picked it up and listened. After a few seconds she hung up.

"The captain requests the honour of our presence in the ship's infirmary."

David looked baffled. "Why?"

"I'm just the intermediary. I have no idea. He said he would explain everything when we get there," Diana replied.

"How very intriguing." Arthur rose to his feet. "Di, are you feeling up to this? We could go without you and let you rest for a while."

"Like hell you will."

Being as it was David's fourth time to the infirmary, he pretty much knew the way by heart. The trip below only took ten minutes that time. The door was locked when they got there but after a gentle knock, an officer opened it and let them enter.

"They're in the exam room." He gestured to the end of the hall. Diana and David knew the room all too well. It was where they had watched the ship's doctor dissolve in front of their eyes.

Three people were waiting for them. The captain introduced the new arrivals to the others. They were the ship's nurse, Sue Barfield, and a passenger, Eldon White. Eldon was a retired doctor who must have been at least eighty years old. His hands showed a slight tremor as they waved off the idea of any handshakes.

"I'm sorry to disturb you all, but Doctor White said something in passing which resonated with me. He mentioned that it was a great shame that we didn't have someone on board who was qualified to do a serious evaluation of an infected patient's blood. Obviously, it will have to be drawn before their body disintegrates. I, of course, thought of you, Mr Olson, and of you, Mr Easton. I believe you are both qualified to carry out such an evaluation."

"In a laboratory setting, with all the necessary equipment, yes," Arthur replied. "I don't know what we could do out here in the middle of the ocean."

"I know it's not ideal, but they do have a top-notch microscope and some decent, though basic, testing equipment," Doctor White advised. "It's more for things like diagnosing the cause of gastric distress or even a viral throat infection in an extreme case, but it's enough for you to be able to detect a blatant anomaly. I would love to be able to do the testing myself but I'm afraid that between my Parkinson's and cataracts, I would probably do more harm than good."

"The thought is for Nurse Barfield to be on call for any reported instance of the green plague," the captain advised. "The hope is to get to the patient in time to draw blood from an unaffected part of the body before it is completely consumed."

"That's not going to be as easy as it sounds," David said. "It seems to take about thirty minutes max from first indication to the end. From what we've been hearing, it's possible that that time frame is getting even shorter."

"We know," the captain said. "We will be advising the entire crew to be on constant lookout for any afflicted individual."

"What if it's a passenger? How is Nurse Barfield to go about obtaining permission to draw blood?" Arthur asked.

"The individuals will not be given a choice, I'm afraid. I will take full responsibility should there later be any legal ramifications. As you all know, as captain I am able to implement and adapt any law in the event of a shipboard emergency."

He studied the others in the room to make sure they were all in agreement with the plan. There were no detractors.

"I will leave you to get set up. I will be on the bridge but will make myself fully available should you need anything from me," Havelin announced.

After the captain was gone, Doctor White looked on as Arthur and David emptied every single cupboard and drawer in the infirmary so as to try and put together some sort of blood testing protocol. The doctor had been correct about the inventory of test equipment. For a ship at sea, it wasn't a bad collection. From a pharmaceutical laboratory perspective, it was pretty much bare-bones but then again, they weren't trying to create a cure, just get some clue as to what they were up against.

The infirmary had a large stock of sterile syringes, needles, pipettes, Petri dishes and glass slides for the microscope. There was a decent stock of blood sample vials and even a small centrifuge. Much to their amazement, there was a small sample case of common medical lab reagents in a tiny tabletop freezer.

It certainly wasn't what they were used to having to hand back in New York, but they felt they could make do. After setting up the counter with everything they could possibly need, they decided they were as ready as they could be.

It was then up to the diligence of the crew and the ability of Nurse Barfield to get to the designated area fast enough. Everyone made a dash back to their respective rooms to gather whatever personal items they needed in order to stay in the infirmary for as long as it took until a potential patient was spotted. They wanted to be prepared for the possibility of a lengthy wait.

It took less than an hour for the first case to appear.

A crew member working in boiler room two felt a tingling feeling in his left foot. He removed his shoe and sock and saw the tell-tale green-black mass. Word was passed up the chain until it reached the nurse. She ran the entire way down to the boiler room but by the time she reached the boilerman, the necrosis was already at his neck. She stood by and watched as his body disintegrated into the overheated boiler-room air.

It was the first green plague death she had seen. She was badly shaken, as were the man's co-workers.

The testing team realised at that point that the ship was simply too big for one person to be the sole responder. Diana immediately volunteered to be the second on-call blood taker. Nurse Barfield gave her a crash course on how to carry out the procedure. Diana was to be staged in the captain's cabin and Nurse Barfield would remain in the infirmary. Buoyed by the challenge, Doctor White also volunteered to join the blood-taking team.

"I might be pretty much useless at everything else, but I most certainly can do something as basic as taking a blood sample," Doctor White nodded enthusiastically. "The one caveat, though, is that I should probably only go for a patient in relatively close proximity to the infirmary. I am regretfully about twenty years past being able to gather too much speed."

They all graciously accepted his offer of help.

The other obvious issue was one of the ship's command structure. Had the boilerman contacted the team directly, they may have reached him in time. Maritime tradition and protocol dictated that in any emergency, a crew member was only to report up to the next senior person.

For a boilerman to reach the testing team, who were classified as captain level, eight different people had to be contacted up the chain. One at a time.

That was changed immediately. All crew were given the direct-dial number of the infirmary and were told to dial it themselves without the need to go through their superior.

The captain gave his approval for the change but couldn't remember an occasion when the rigid reporting structure of a maritime vessel had been so completely undermined. He was dubious of the results, but willing to give it a try considering the gravity of the current situation.

The next call came two hours later. A woman on the aft sun deck had been reported as having the tell-tale signs by a deck steward. Nurse Barfield headed topside. Only minutes after she departed, another call came in that a passenger in second class had been swimming in the indoor pool when he noticed his feet turning black. A steward called the direct line and Diana rushed off to tend to the man.

David and Arthur reviewed their planned procedure while they waited.

Nurse Barfield called down from the sun deck and advised that it had been a false sighting. The woman in question had a rather large, dark birthmark on her left thigh. It was not necrosis and the passenger was furious at all the unwanted attention that had been focused upon her. The group in the infirmary couldn't help but laugh. Their nerves were so taut that any levity was cause for some release.

The mood quickly changed moments later when a seaman staggered into the infirmary, holding up an infected shipmate. His shoes and socks were gone and his trousers were rolled up to the knee. The necrosis had already covered the parts of his legs that were visible.

David ushered the men into one of the small treatment rooms and Arthur cut away the rest of the infected crewman's clothing. The green plague had passed his midriff and was climbing towards his chest. Arthur grabbed a syringe and was about to tear off the protective paper wrap when Doctor White stepped into the room.

"May I?" he asked in a professional tone.

Arthur handed him the syringe and needle. The doctor's hands were shaking, but he still managed to undo the sanitised wrap and attach the needle to the syringe. He turned to the young man.

"Be strong, son. This won't hurt."

He chose a spot at the join of the neck and shoulders. He realised he'd forgotten something and returned to the prep table. He grabbed a cotton ball and poured alcohol onto it. The necrosis was now at the man's collarbone.

"You might have to find a higher spot," David suggested.

"This will be fine," White assured him as he dabbed the alcohol on the man's skin.

Doctor White had the needle poised but couldn't seem to immediately find a vein. He tapped a few places but still wasn't satisfied.

He didn't seem to be aware that the green-black mass was only an inch below where he was prodding.

"There it is," he announced proudly.

He inserted the needle. As he started to draw the blood, the necrosis reached the site of the needle.

Doctor White tried to draw the blood but instead drew up a blackish liquid. The syringe started to fill. There was the sound of glass cracking.

The syringe crumbled in his hand covering him in the slimy black ooze. As he and the others watched, Doctor White's own hands became necrotic. It spread across his body with frightening speed.

"Oh my. This is something new," he said as he watched the mass devour him. It reached his head within seconds, at which point, there was a final puff of green then his clothes collapsed in a pile on the floor. Next to the doctor's unneeded garments, the original patient whose blood the retired doctor had attempted to draw, watched the old man disintegrate. His eyes showed his fear until they too were consumed. The patient and Doctor White had both disappeared into the ether, only moments apart.

"Dear Jesus," Arthur whispered.

"Let's get out of this room," David suggested.

Once in the hall, the two men stared frantically at each other. They had to make sure that none of the tainted blood that had triggered the doctor's death had landed on either of them.

Once they realised that they were both in the clear they leant against the passageway wall and both bowed their heads as a result of fear, emotion and mental exhaustion.

They were startled out of their silence by Diana charging into the infirmary. She was soaking wet. She held out a blood sample in a rubber-corked test tube. She looked very pleased with herself.

"Got some!" she said.

The two men looked at the test tube with grave concern. Arthur gently took it from her hand and looked upon it, with a mix of awe and respect.

"It wasn't easy," she announced. "The guy refused to get out of the pool. We had to hold him still in the shallow end so that I could draw the blood."

"Did he – you know?" David asked.

"Die?" She looked at him askance at his inability to say the words.

"Yes – die."

"He did. In water, it's even stranger. The final green puff coloured the pool for a few moments before disappearing. Everyone panicked and tried to swim away from it."

"We had a new twist here, as well. Doctor White tried to draw blood and accidently drew it just as the necrosis reached the needle. It shattered the syringe and covered his hands."

"Oh my god. Is he all right?" she asked.

"No, honey," Arthur replied. "The necrotic blood somehow supercharged the process. He was consumed within seconds."

"Is mine safe?" She held out the test tube.

"It looks to me to be normal blood. Let's find out." Her father took the blood sample from her then headed for the main exam room. The others started to follow.

"I think you should let me open this alone, just in case."

"Dad! No!"

"It's just a precaution. I'll be very careful," Arthur assured her.

He stepped through the double doors at the end of the passageway then closed them behind him.

"How are you doing?" David asked her.

"I lost my mother a few hours ago. My father is about to uncork blood that could kill him in seconds and I just stood in a swimming pool watching someone dissolve. I'd have to say David, that I've had better days."

They stood in the passageway for almost half an hour. Every so often, one of them called out to make sure Arthur was still alive. Each time, he responded that everything was going well.

The double doors suddenly opened and Arthur gestured for them to join him.

"David, have a look in the microscope and tell me what you see."

David leaned over the device and looked at the slide that was already in place. He was puzzled. He increased the magnification.

"So, what do you see?" Arthur asked.

"Red blood cells, white blood cells, platelets and, of course, plasma," David advised.

"Does it look normal to you?"

"Not remotely. All the elements of normal blood are there, but…" David tried to find the right words.

"But what, David?"

"What I'm seeing looks like a photograph. Each cell is too perfect. The entire image is too pristine. Blood doesn't look like that. Plus, and this is the incredible part, there is no movement. The smear is obviously fresh, so the cells should be in motion. A blood slide is not a still life. It should be teeming with activity. There is nothing alive in this blood sample."

"Nicely put, David." Arthur patted his arm.

"I wonder if the necrosis affects the blood prior to the destruction of the entire body. Maybe the victim's blood dies just before the rest of him – or her," David suggested.

"That would certainly be an interesting hypothesis if it weren't for one small detail," Arthur added.

"What's that?"

"The sample you just looked at came from me."

"Daddy!" Diana shouted. "What the hell were you doing?"

"When I examined the blood that Di brought back from the pool, I saw the same lifeless image. I decided I needed to take a sample from myself so we could have a direct comparator. Imagine my surprise when I found that my blood also appeared motionless."

"May I look?" Diana asked.

David stepped away from the microscope. Diana stared at the slide for a long time, before looking at the others.

"There must be some other explanation. You can't be alive if your blood is dead – can you?"

CHAPTER
FOURTEEN

Once they had cleaned up the testing area, Diana and her father decided to visit the ship's chapel to find out the shipboard procedure for arranging a small service for Myra. Arthur had initially wanted to continue examining the blood sample but his daughter's glare made it clear that he was to accompany her.

David suggested that he go with them but Diana felt that, considering her mother's opinion of him, even if her mother wasn't there physically, there was something karmatically wrong with him being there.

He couldn't argue that point. As he made his way to his cabin, he realised that he was surprisingly hungry. He'd only picked at breakfast and that had been over eight hours ago.

He made his way up to the snack bar by the main pool on Sun Deck. As he stepped outside from the stair lobby he saw the teens from the other night. They had encircled an elderly man and were trying to manhandle him towards the railing.

Their intent was obvious. The poor man was to be thrown to the fog. He didn't seem to be suffering from the plague but he looked to be very old, frail and terrified.

David shouted at the pack to stop what they were doing immediately. He looked about the pool area hoping to find support from others. The entire area was deserted. As David looked with surprise at the usually packed pool deck, he saw the entire area morph into something far less inviting. The pool was now covered in a dark green growth. The decoratively tiled walls of the swimming pool had collapsed inwards into piles of wet rubble. Sea vegetation had grown over the mound. The surrounding teak decks were buckled and black with rot.

The vision suddenly cleared. David saw that the teens had turned from the old man and were facing him. He could see immediately that they were all sick. Their faces and any other exposed skin were mottled with necrosis, yet it didn't seem to be spreading. Their eyes which had been so unnaturally bright when he'd last seen them, were now dull and lifeless.

They stood immobile and stared at David without saying a word.

"Leave this man alone. He's done nothing to you."

David looked down at the old man and tried to give him a comforting look.

The old man had transformed into a putrid corpse. He looked to have been dead for a long time. Bones poked through heavily decomposed flesh. His chest had been torn open and very little remained inside. His clothing, at least what little remained, had rotted and melded with his rancid bodily fluids.

David looked to the teens. They were gone. They had vanished into thin air. David stepped back away from what was left of the old man. The last thing he saw before forcing himself to turn away was a large, pale deep-water crab crawling out of the man's gaping chest cavity. In one claw, it held part of a torn rib. A piece of putrefied flesh still clung to the decayed piece of bone.

David closed his eyes, determined not to retch.

"May I get you something, sir? A cocktail? Perhaps a sandwich?"

David opened his eyes. The deck steward that had served him and Diana the other day was looking at him with just a trace of concern. David looked back down at the deck. There was no sign of the old man.

"Perhaps if you'd just like to sit here and relax..." the steward offered as he gestured to a deckchair a few feet away. "I could get you something to pick you up a bit. How about a Bloody Mary? You like them spicy, if memory serves me correctly."

David could only nod, then plopped himself down on the chair at which point the steward headed off to get his drink. David took a couple of deep breaths then looked around the pool area. It wasn't as crowded as other days but there were a couple of dozen passengers having drinks and sandwiches while others were playing and splashing in the crystal-clear pool water. It all looked very normal.

Something caught his eye by the ship's railing. He turned his head just in time to see a large crab slip under one of the safely lines and vanish over the side. It had been carrying something in its left claw. It looked like a piece of putrefied flesh hanging from the end of a rib bone.

Diana and her father sat at the back of the chapel. It was designed to be multi-denominational so there were no trappings of any one religion. Even so, the hundred-seat room had an aura of peace, tranquillity and safety. They were alone with the exception of one woman seated in the front row. She was wearing a headscarf and was reciting the rosary in an almost inaudible whisper.

Diana and Arthur hadn't been able to find the chaplain, but found that just being in that serene space was enough to help them fondly remember Myra and be able to say a more formal goodbye.

After about half an hour they looked at each other to gauge whether any more time was needed. They were both red-eyed but nodded that they were done. They had said their farewells.

They slid out of their row and made for the polished pine doors.

"Where should we have lunch today?" a voice called out.

They turned back into the chapel but could only see the back of the woman in the front row.

"Excuse me, ma'am?" Arthur asked. "Did you say something?"

The woman turned to face them. Myra Olson gave them a huge smile.

"Yes. I was wondering as to our lunch plans. I'm feeling quite peckish. Just please don't tell me that that dreadful young man will be joining us. I've been through enough already."

Diana had never fainted in her life. In fact, she never understood how such an embarrassing thing could even happen. She just managed to get her rear onto the edge of the nearest pew, then passed out cold, lengthwise on the hard wooden bench. Arthur's reaction was completely different. He screamed like a small child.

David downed his Bloody Mary in one, then with a mildly embarrassed expression, ordered a second one and a club sandwich. As he drank and ate he studied those around him for any signs of contagion. They all seemed to be both in good health and in good spirits.

The one thing that gave him pause was that the grey fog had changed colour slightly. It was still grey, but now had a distinct green tinge to it. It also seemed to have become slightly translucent, though he couldn't quite see into it.

As he finished his lunch, he noticed that a small crowd had gathered by the entry to the interior stairwell. They seemed to have surrounded somebody.

He walked by, trying not to appear too nosey. He could hear the crowd peppering the poor individual with questions. David finally got close enough to squeeze between two large women and was able to see who they were all talking to.

David felt his legs turn to rubber. In the midst of the crowd stood the ship's doctor wearing a white terrycloth bathrobe. Dr Williams was trying to answer as many questions as he could. He noticed David and gave him a knowing nod. For a moment their eyes met.

David found himself staring into the same eyes that he had watched being consumed by the green plague.

They were bright blue and seemed to sparkle in the early afternoon light.

He would have looked completely normal were it not for the patch of black necrotic tissue on the side of his neck.

The doctor pushed his way through the crowd and stood smiling at David.

"Surprised to see me?"

"Considering we watched you die, yes. Very surprised."

"I guess that is understandable," the doctor said. "I can promise you one thing. I am far more surprised than you to be back among the living. I had always believed that once you died, that was pretty much it."

"Do you remember what happened to you?" David whispered.

"Yes and no. I remember watching the necrosis consume my body and knew that I was about to die, but I don't remember much after that."

"But you remember something?"

"Yes." The doctor stepped closer to David. "I have a vivid memory of looking at you looking at me. You and your young lady seemed deeply pained. I am very sorry to have put you both through that."

"Do you have any thoughts as to how you've managed to return from the dead?" David meant his words to sound serious, but realised that they seemed more like something from a horror movie.

"None whatsoever," he replied. "I just found myself standing by the railing a few minutes ago, just over there."

He pointed to a spot about a hundred feet further aft from where they were standing.

"Are you feeling all right?" David asked.

"I was initially a little embarrassed. When I returned, if that's the right term, I was stark naked. A passenger had to lend me their robe. Other than that, I am feeling in particularly fine fettle. I am a bit concerned about the dead patches though. I'm not sure that they will improve my chances of any onboard romances."

David laughed. "You might be interested to know that at the captain's request, Diana's father and I set up a testing station in the infirmary. Would you mind if we checked you out and took a little blood?"

"I think that's absolutely essential. I myself would love to know what magic serum is running through my reincarnated body. I was planning to have a gander myself but let's all have a peek."

The doctor headed for the stairway lobby. He held the door open for David. He looked like an excited child that was about to open a surprise gift.

"Perhaps you might want to put on a little more clothing," David suggested.

The doctor looked down at the robe. A blush rose to his cheeks.

"Damn good suggestion." He started down the stairs.

CHAPTER
FIFTEEN

David told the doctor that he would meet him in the infirmary. He wanted to check on Diana first. He was pretty sure they would have finished making funeral arrangements in the chapel, so he headed directly to their suite.

Their door was slightly ajar. He poked his head in the entry hall.

"Is everyone decent?" he called out.

"Come on in," Arthur replied. "We have a little bit of good news. Leave the door open. We ordered some snacks from room service."

"I have some interesting news as well," David exclaimed proudly.

"I'm relatively certain that our news will trump yours." Diana gave him a huge hug as he entered the main salon.

"That's where you're wrong. Guess who I saw?"

"Just what we don't need! Does he have to be here?" Myra Olson asked as she stepped out of the master cabin. She glared at him as if he were some insect that had dared to enter her living space.

David could only stare. Diana's mother looked completely healthy save for two patches of dead tissue. One was on her neck, the other started on her right cheek and covered the top half of her nose.

"It's very rude to stare," Myra said.

"You're alive!" David managed.

"Well done, Mr Easton. That little deduction must have exhausted you." She turned to Diana. "I am terribly happy for you, my dear. He really is quite a catch."

"You promised you'd be nice," Diana scolded.

"I've had my say," Myra added. "What I need now is a drink. Darling, where's that room service you promised?"

"I only ordered it fifteen minutes ago," Arthur replied patiently. "I'm sure it will be here soon."

"May I ask you a rather unusual question, Mrs Olson?" David asked hesitantly.

"If you must."

"Where did you find yourself when you... returned?"

"I'm not sure why you want to know, but it was on Sun Deck by the railing," Myra replied.

"Was there anything unusual about your situation?"

"Other than the fact that I had died and was suddenly reborn?" she asked.

"Yes. Other than that." David tried to remain tactful.

"I think reincarnation was definitely the only really unusual occurrence."

"May I enquire how you were dressed when you returned?"

"Oh that!" Myra laughed. "I was absolutely stark naked. I had to steal a pool towel from a deckchair so I could get back to the suite."

"David," Arthur sounded serious, "haven't we already talked about the nudity thing when it comes to my wife?"

"It wasn't me this time," David declared, terrified that Arthur was actually upset. One look at his face showed that he had been teasing him. David sighed with relief.

There was a knock on the suite door.

"Room service," a familiar voice called out.

David walked back to the entry hall and saw Andrew, his old cabin steward, wheeling a large silver trolley into the suite.

"You're alive," David said.

"I am indeed, Mr Easton. Funny thing is – folks that passed over the last few days are popping up like spring daffodils. I hope I didn't cause you any distress with my absence."

"I'm just happy to see you back with us," David said.

David was trying to find the patch of necrotic tissue on the steward but couldn't see any. Andrew could see that David was trying, albeit subtly, to find something.

"I think you may be looking for this, sir." Andrew turned his back on David and pulled down his collar. The area just below his hairline on the back of his neck was greenish-black. "Everyone who's come back has at least one somewhere. It's like our badge of honour."

David lowered his voice. "Does it hurt?"

"Not at all, sir," he replied.

"Do you remember anything about your passing or your return?"

"Not a thing, sir. I remember first seeing the thing growing up my leg and then going to the infirmary. That's when you saw me. I went back to work and remember putting on another pot of coffee in the pantry. The next thing I remember was finding myself on deck by the aft railing earlier this morning. Funny thing was, I was naked as the day I was born. Very embarrassing, it was."

"Steward, please ignore Mr Easton if you don't mind and continue with service," Myra called out from the salon.

Andrew gave David a raised-eyebrow smile then resumed pushing the trolley.

David followed closely behind then approached Arthur.

"The ship's doctor has also returned and is waiting for us in the infirmary," David announced. "I said we'd want to examine his blood."

"I think that takes precedence over a glass of champagne at this point," Arthur stated as he faced the others. "If you'll excuse David and me for a few minutes, we have to pop down to the infirmary to run one quick test."

"Your wife returns from the dead and you have something more important to attend to?" Myra asked in complete amazement.

"Actually, yes," Arthur replied. "As much as we all feel blessed that you are back with us – we need to find out how and why that miracle occurred."

"Do what you must." Myra dismissed him.

"Do you need my help?" Diana asked.

"No. You stay here and keep an eye on your mother. Don't let her disappear again," Arthur smiled.

Doctor Williams was waiting for them when they arrived in the infirmary. He was wearing his usual dress whites. He had saved the others some time and taken his own blood sample. Though he felt perfectly capable of doing so, he let the specialists create their own slides. Once he'd seen his own blood being drawn up into the syringe, he'd immediately known that there was something amiss.

He sat calmly on a tall counter stool and watched David and Arthur as they entered the temporary lab. He held out the blood vial.

David held it up to the light as both he and Arthur looked at the doctor's blood.

"Did you just draw this blood?" Arthur asked.

"Yes. Just a few seconds ago," the doctor replied.

"And you haven't mixed it with anything?" David stared at the vial in amazement.

"Not a thing."

"Then why the hell does your blood look like sea water?"

After creating a number of slides, David handed the small slide rack to Arthur, who mounted the first one under the microscope's stage clips.

They both took turns looking at the sample.

"The slide must have been dirty," David suggested after looking through the microscope.

"It came from an unopened sterile pack," Arthur said.

"What's wrong? You both look as if you'd seen something otherworldly," the doctor observed. "May I remind you both that I have recently been totally consumed by some necrotic fungus and then popped up alive again a day later. I'm not sure what you could possibly find that could be deemed unusual at this point."

Arthur stood away from the microscope to let the doctor have a look for himself.

The ship's doctor leant over the device and lowered his eyes to the ocular lens.

"What the dickens is going on in my blood?" he whispered. "That is if it can be called blood at all."

"That's exactly our concern," David replied.

The doctor took another longer look. He slowly shook his head.

"I don't appear to have any red blood cells. That's a little unusual."

"What do you think about what appears to have replaced them?" Arthur asked. "Have you ever seen anything like that before?"

"Can't say that I have. Whatever those things are, they seem quite healthy. They're dashing all over the place."

David took another look. He felt that he had seen the strange, elongated single cell objects somewhere before. They now made up a large portion of the man's blood.

"I have to go to the ship's library," David announced.

"I've got all the top medical books next door in my cabin," Williams said.

"I'm not looking for a medical book." David gave them both a forced smile then left the room.

He got to the library in record time. He was amazed to find dozens of passengers all looking through a variety of medical reference books. All the passengers had the dead skin marks. They were among the newly reanimated.

He doubted they were going to find too many books that referenced returning from the dead. At least not in the medical section.

David wasn't interested in any of the medical books. His research was in an entirely different science.

He walked back into the infirmary with a large coffee-table book under his arm. The front cover showed a colourful ocean floor alive with sea creatures of every imaginable size and shape.

He placed it on the testing counter. The other two gave him confused looks.

He opened the book to a folded page showing dozens of pictures of bizarre-looking microscopic sea creatures. He tapped his finger on one particular photo halfway down the page.

"May I introduce you gentlemen to my new friend – and yours, Doctor. Please meet Xanthophytes. If I'm not mistaken, these are what has replaced all of your red blood cells."

The three studied the picture. The creatures looked like fuzzy green hot dogs on skewers.

"That does look like what we saw. What is it? Some sort of virus?" Arthur asked.

"No. It's nano plankton," David explained. "A very small form of algae."

Williams couldn't take his eyes off the picture. "You mean it's common in blood?"

"Oh, god no! That I'm afraid is a complete aberration. It's a form of sea plankton found at extreme depths. We're talking below 25,000 feet. Your blood appears to now be full of the things."

The doctor looked anxiously at the others.

"In that case… how the hell am I alive?"

They left a highly puzzled Doctor Williams in his infirmary while they made their way to the captain's cabin. They felt he should hear about these new anomalies directly.

"Can a person be alive with blood like that?" David asked Arthur as they waited by a crew elevator.

"I would normally say no. That's not how the body was designed to work, but you saw my blood. It had the right parts but seemed inanimate. The doctor's blood, on the other hand, seemed very alive, just with the wrong things. I think the time has come for us to acknowledge that we are way out of our depth here. No pun intended."

The elevator doors opened and they saw the first officer standing facing them. He looked shaken.

"Commander Hess. We were just coming up to speak with the captain," Arthur stated.

Hess stared at him as if he'd suggested something inconceivable.

"I suppose that would be acceptable," he answered almost reluctantly.

Hess led them to the captain's cabin. As they approached the door, it swung open and Captain Havelin eyed his surprise visitors with disappointment.

"I thought you might be my communications officer."

"Has there been a change?" Arthur asked.

"Apparently so. I was just heading to the wireless room. Did you wish to speak with me?"

"Yes, sir. It will only take a minute."

"You'd better come in." As he turned to step back into his room, they both saw the necrotic patch on his lower neck.

"Commander, please advise the wireless room that I will be bringing guests through in ten minutes."

"Sir," Hess acknowledged.

David closed the cabin door. "When did it happen, sir?"

The captain seemed about to pretend to not understand their question.

"We are fully aware that people are coming back after being consumed. We have spent the last hour or so with three such people. One of them is the ship's doctor," Arthur explained.

"Williams has come back?" The captain seemed pleased. "That's good. We need him."

He sat heavily in an armchair. "I am told that I expired shortly after we last talked. I returned less than thirty minutes ago."

"David and I have been running some blood tests on those about to expire and in Doctor Williams' case, someone who has just returned. The findings are – well, they're basically inexplicable."

"Try to explain it anyway, if you would be so kind. I feel I should be privy to the facts even if they are incomprehensible or impossible."

"I should also mention that I tested my own blood," Arthur advised. "It would seem that anyone prior to succumbing to the plague appears to have what I can only describe as inanimate blood. David put it best. He said it looks like a photo of blood. Then after the reanimation…"

"Is that a clinical term, Mr Olson?"

"No, Captain. As it's never happened before in a non-biblical setting, it was the best I could come up with on the spur of the moment."

The captain nodded. "Reanimation. Hmm. I like it."

Arthur continued to describe what they'd found in the doctor's blood. The captain asked a few basic questions about blood then threw the big question at them.

"Are you therefore theorising that we are not alive?"

"No. I'm not. It's very apparent that we are very much alive. It's not what flows within our body that makes us what we are. It's our sentient capacity. To quote Descartes 'I think, therefore I am'. We are definitely living, but appear to be mutating. I have no proof to offer you, but I'm even more convinced that it has something to do with the fog."

"Can you postulate that conviction into something a little more clarifying?" Havelin asked.

"No, sir. I cannot." Arthur looked to David. "Mr Easton – any thoughts?"

"None, except that everything that has happened began with the fog. By the way. If you haven't yet noticed, it's starting to change colour."

"I hadn't noticed. Then again, I've been away, so to speak. I'm not really that shocked, however. Everything else is going completely cockeyed." The captain rubbed his chin. "Tell me, gentlemen – do you clearly recall the period before the fog? Do you even remember in detail our departure from New York?"

"Of course," David answered. "We... I know that... I just can't quite…"

"Recall it?" Havelin suggested.

Arthur and David stared at the captain as a chill seemed to settle within the cabin.

"Hmm. That's what I thought," Havelin voiced. "I can't recall anything either. I have checked with other officers who all say the same thing."

"So, what does that mean?" David asked.

"Mr Easton… I have absolutely no bloody idea whatsoever. In fact, I have lost track of exactly how much I no longer understand on board this ship. That is not a good position for a captain to be in."

Arthur and David stared at him with growing concern.

"Anyway," Havelin continued, "I'm glad you showed up when you did so that I can share the latest shipboard anomaly with you. Care to join me in the wireless room? It's quite a place. State of the art. There's no ship with better equipment afloat today."

"Except that nobody seems to be able to hear us," David sighed.

CHAPTER
SIXTEEN

The wireless room was one deck up and a couple of hundred feet aft. It was located within the deck housing that surrounded funnel number one. It was spread between two heavily secured rooms. One was about twice the size of David's cabin and was home to six telephony and telegraphy operators. There seemed to be four distinct work areas within the space. Against one wall was a giant patch-corded telephonic switchboard. It was for shipboard communications only.

Two women in matching blue and white uniforms were busy patching call after call across the ship. Sharing the same wall was a much smaller switchboard separated by a wooden partition. A uniformed man was holding a normal-looking telephone handset that was attached to a large black wireless device. Next to that was what looked like a small typewriter. Above him, on a wall shelf, stood two more black boxes covered in dials and knobs. The captain explained that it was the ship-to-shore wireless radio station. On the opposite wall stood a maple desktop that spanned the length of the room. On one end were a pair of keyboards for typing telegrams. Two young men wearing the same blue and white uniforms were typing up the messages from yellow passenger telegram requests.

At the far end of the room was a small, unmanned workstation. On it sat an old-fashioned-looking wood-boxed radio and a Morse code telegraph sounder and receiver.

A young officer stood in the middle of the room attentively watching his team at work. The captain made the introductions.

"We are still sending all messages and attempting radio phone connections as if everything was still working," the captain whispered. "Until such time as we know for certain that nothing is getting through, we will keep this room fully operational."

"Except for that station?" Arthur gestured to the telegraph sounder.

"Actually, we still send a message from there at various times during the day. It's a very low-powered system and at most has been known to reach just over 200 miles. We feel that that's the least likely signal to get through the fog, but we try anyway."

Havelin turned to the communications officer. "I believe you have something for me to hear?"

"Yes, sir, though it's more your eyes that I need for this demonstration." He stepped over to the telegraphy team. He picked up a black box that seemed to have what looked like a small TV screen at the front. He plugged it into the side of one of the metal boxes.

"If you'd care to watch the screen." He pushed a button on the box with the screen. It flickered to life showing a backlit grey screen.

The captain watched intently.

"What you will see is the outgoing radio waves carrying the plain text transmission," the communications officer explained.

He then looked down at one of the operators. "Please continue typing as before." The man resumed his work.

As he typed, the grey screen filled with radio waves confirming the outgoing transmission.

"I'm now going to plug the oscilloscope into the receiving station."

The officer plugged the screen into a different black box then nodded at the operator. As he typed, the same sine waves appeared on the screen but they were fuzzy and even occasionally doubled.

The captain's expression changed to one of confusion. "What am I seeing here?"

"What you are seeing is our outgoing signal bouncing straight back to us. We shouldn't see any return sound waves except in the case of a response from the intended destination, or even a new message arriving from some other source."

David turned to the communications officer. "Your signal is bouncing back roughly a couple of microseconds after transmission. Its modulation and frequency are also slightly out of phase."

The captain looked to his communications officer to see if he agreed with David.

"Very impressive, Mr Easton. That's exactly what we see," the officer agreed.

"You got all that from those curvy lines?" Arthur sounded impressed.

David shrugged his shoulders.

"When exactly did the rebound signals start?" Havelin asked.

"About six hours ago. We assumed it was something wrong with our equipment but after testing every single component, we realised that it wasn't a fault on board."

"So, what does it mean?" the captain asked.

"As none of us has ever seen anything like it we can only surmise, but it seems to confirm that none of our signals are getting to their destination. They seem to only get as far as the fog," the officer stated.

"That's one hell of a supposition."

The officer nodded. "It is indeed, sir."

"Keep me posted, please," the captain requested. The frustration was evident in his tone.

"Yes, sir."

"While we are here, I get the feeling that our guests might like to see the equipment room. Would you mind?" Havelin asked.

"It would be my pleasure, sir," the officer replied.

He led the captain, Arthur and David out of the operations room and into the second door just down the passageway. David was amazed. He loved to tinker with consumer-level radios and radio kits. As a child he had been addicted to Heath Kit electronic build-your-own model kits. He thought he'd seen just about every system set-up there was.

What he saw now took his breath away. The room was over fifty feet long and nearly as wide. It was filled with amplifiers, pre-amps, power adaptors, emergency power supplies, signal boosters, oscilloscopes, signal modulation units – the list went on and on.

The captain saw the joy on David's face. "Impressive, isn't it?"

"I have a HAM radio unit at home that I'm quite proud of. At least I was," David said. "This is simply amazing."

"As I said – state of the art. Some of this equipment isn't even available yet. We're testing a few new components to see if we should have them on all our vessels."

"That signal booster over there; I've read about it but have never seen one." David was almost drooling.

"Well spotted. It's not scheduled for production until mid-sixty-three. We got it a year ahead of time so we could put it through its paces in a real-world environment."

"How's that working so far?" Arthur asked with a trace of sarcasm.

"We remain hopeful," Havelin replied.

"Captain, if I may, what is your plan at this point?" David asked.

"Specific to any one issue, or the situation as a whole?"

"Let's go with the situation as a whole," David replied.

The captain turned to his communications officer. "Would you give us a few minutes, please?"

"Sir." He acknowledged the request, then left the three alone in the equipment room.

"Let's consider the facts for a moment," Captain Havelin began. "We seem to have no steering control. We have no ability to communicate with the outside world. I, like many others, have recently died then been... reanimated, if I may use your term. Parts of the ship seem to be deteriorating and as you have just reported, everyone on board seems to no longer have viable blood within their bodies. I am highly dubious that anything we may choose to do at this point will change the current situation. In case it hasn't dawned on you, we are no longer in control here. Without wishing to sound remotely flippant, we seem to only be along for the ride, so to speak."

"Are you saying you're not planning to do anything?" Arthur asked. "You're just going to sit back and watch?"

"Not at all. Myself and my crew are trying to tackle every new crisis as it arises. We are trying to determine the cause of every abnormal event that has occurred. That said – in case you haven't noticed, everything that has occurred is not physically possible in any reality of which I am aware. If either of you feel that you can add any semblance of an idea as to how we should proceed, please speak freely."

"Have you considered using one of your cargo booms to take someone into the fog?" David suggested. "At least we may learn something about it."

The captain stared at him, long and hard. "You truly are a most unusual man, Mr Easton. I don't believe we have contemplated such an action. Considering that the fog seems to be directly linked to everything that's occurred, I have to say that I feel extremely remiss at not having come up with that option myself."

"I think it's fair to say that you have quite a lot on your mind at the moment," Arthur suggested.

"I would like to volunteer to be the one who goes into the fog," David declared.

"David! Think about what you are suggesting," Arthur said.

"As captain, I can't and won't intentionally place one of my passengers in such a dangerous situation."

"Sir, with all due respect, we are already in a highly dangerous situation. I really can't imagine that anything worse could befall me while examining the fog that couldn't strike me down right here on board ship."

"Still, I feel this task should fall to a crew member," Havelin insisted. "There is nothing that you can offer that one of my crew couldn't match or top. They are highly trained, fit, and dedi..."

"Do they have a PhD in microbiology?" David interrupted. "Whatever the substance of that fog is, I am in a better position to take samples and even postulate the structure and make-up of the thing. We keep calling it a fog. You and I both know that that is the one thing it is not. I don't think we can make determinations on how to save this ship and all aboard her, unless we learn what that thing out there is really made of. I believe that I am your best option for finding that out."

The captain studied the younger man. He prayed that he wasn't about to send him to his death. Then again, he wasn't exactly clear on the definition of death any more.

CHAPTER
SEVENTEEN

The captain met with his first officer as soon as he returned from the wireless room. Commander Hess was given full responsibility for the operation to get David into the fog.

While Hess worked with his deck and cargo officers, David went below to the infirmary to prep some sterile sponges and test tubes with stoppers that he planned to use to obtain samples of the environment.

As he was packing his meagre kit into a sealable plastic bag, Diana stormed into the prep room.

"What the hell do you think you're doing? You can't go out there. The captain specifically told you that a crew member would do it. Stop this hero nonsense. I want you around a little longer."

"I'm going to be in a full wetsuit with oxygen. I'll be fine," he insisted.

"That's a load of crap and you know it. You have absolutely zero idea of what's out there. Let some other schmuck risk their life," Diana raged. "There are almost 3,000 people on this ship who I care nothing about. Let one of them go."

"Did you just say you cared?"

"Stop being so needy. Of course I care. I also assume that you feel the same way, so stop all this nonsense and let someone else get dangled out over the damn ocean."

"I'm sorry, but I am the only one who might be able to find out what that fog really is."

"I don't care about the damn fog. In case you weren't listening, I quite like you. I know I'm being selfish, but I want you here – with me."

"The whole thing will take an hour at most. Then we'll have a couple of martinis to celebrate my valiant return." He tilted her chin up with his finger so he could look into her eyes. "Think how proud you'll be when I save the ship." David smiled.

She stared at him as she tried to find the right words.

"Don't you dare get killed out there. If you do, I swear I will never, ever forgive you," she said.

He kissed her gently, then grabbed his kit. "See you on deck."

She watched him exit the infirmary. Every molecule of her being wanted to run after him.

"Ass!" she whispered to herself as she felt her eyes begin to tear up.

A crewman met David by a forward bulkhead that led to the foredeck and escorted him to where a small team had gathered.

David was helped into a thick rubber wetsuit. It was heavy and severely restricted his range of motion.

"I can't wear this. I'd be better with just a swimsuit."

"You'll wear the protective equipment or you won't go at all," Commander Hess advised.

"I'm sure the captain would understand..."

"The captain fully understands, Mr Easton," Captain Havelin said as he joined the gathering. "Commander Hess and I have already discussed this. It's irregular enough to have a passenger undertake such a task, but I sure as hell won't let him do so unprotected."

David could see that any further debate would have been completely futile.

A twin oxygen tank rig was strapped to his back. He could hardly stand under the weight. It was meant to be worn under water where the weight would become more manageable in neutral buoyancy.

The forward cargo boom had already been rigged with a boson's chair suspended from its tip. It took two crew members to get him seated within the contraption.

A dive expert explained the basics of the oxygen regulator. Because he would not be under water and thus not have to endure increased water pressure, the oxygen would last longer. The dive master estimated he would have seventy minutes of air should he need it. He put the mouthpiece between his teeth and tried his first breath. David was reminded to breathe in from the mouth and exhale from the nose. Though it had sounded rudimentary to him, it took David a few breaths to get it right.

He was then handed a dive mask.

"No," he insisted after spitting out the mouthpiece. "There I draw the line. I have to have one hundred per cent clear vision for this to work. The mask could fog, get wet – who knows? Please, Captain. Let me at least have my eyes."

Captain Havelin looked to his first officer to see if he had an opinion. Hess shrugged his shoulders.

"Fine. You may have your eyes," Havelin said. "One last thing, though."

He looped a stainless-steel whistle on the end of a nylon cord over his head. "I was going to insist on a walkie-talkie but with the signal disturbance and the weight of the thing, I knew you'd say no. This is the alternative."

David smiled down at the whistle hanging halfway down his rubber-encased chest.

"If I get in trouble I'll make sure to blow as hard as I can."

"I think it's fair to say that being such a blowhard, that shouldn't be much of a stretch for you," Havelin smirked.

"Why, Captain Havelin – was that an actual joke?" David asked.

"It's a rarity but they do present themselves on occasion."

David replaced the mouthpiece, at which point Hess gave the cargo boom operator the thumbs-up signal and the boom slowly rose thirty feet above the deck. It stopped just before taking up the final slack in the cable attached to the boson's chair.

"You ready?" Havelin asked.

With his mouthpiece in place, all David could do was to give a thumbs-up.

The operator activated the boom winch and the cable began to gently lift David into the air. Once he was ten feet above the deck, the winch stopped. The boom then began to pivot, sending David slowly over the side of the ship.

David had an extraordinary view of the length of the port side of the *Oceanis*. He was astonished to see that every inch of deck space seemed to be crowded with passengers and crew. They were all watching what was undoubtedly one of the strangest sights any of them had ever seen.

The boom continued to swing towards the fog wall. David was only a few feet away. He readied his test tubes and sponges. The audience cheered him on.

David was suddenly terrified. What would he find beyond the grey/green mass? Would he be ripped from the boom and hurled back at the ship? Would his body decompose and disintegrate?

The boom stopped just inches short of the fog. He could see the captain signalling a thumbs-up from the foredeck. David could also see Diana standing a few feet from the officer. She gave him a wave and he could see that she had been crying. He balanced his testing kit with one hand and raised his thumb with the other.

The crowd gasped as David turned away from the ship and faced the fog. The boom then manoeuvred him into the swirling mass.

For a split second, David was surrounded by a greenish-grey mist, then suddenly he was staring back at the *Oceanis* instead of facing away from it.

The crowd cheered, then laughed. David could see the boom where it entered the fog ten feet to his left, yet he was still hanging from the tip of the boom that was poking back out seemingly separated from its other half.

The boom operator tried bringing the boom back towards the ship. David re-entered the fog backwards but was instantly out of it again and was facing the grey-green wall again.

The captain gave the order for one more attempt, but for the boom to be moved at its slowest speed.

The onlookers then got a visual experience they would never forget.

With the boom swinging out in almost slow motion, they were able, albeit for a split second, to see David's backside protruding from the fog as he entered it, right next to his front, as he emerged from it.

As the operator tried the manoeuvre a number of times, David found that if he angled his head the right way, he could just make out his own backside, ten feet away, vanishing into then reappearing from the fog.

The captain ordered the boom be retracted. It was pretty clear that whatever the stuff was, it didn't follow any of the known principles of physics.

As David was gently lowered back to the deck and his diving gear removed, he noticed a small gathering by the operator's hut.

He stepped over, wearing only his swimsuit, and saw a dress white uniform crumpled onto a pair of highly polished shoes. The captain was looking down at the sight with a pained expression.

David stood next to him. "Commander Hess?"

The captain nodded.

"At least we know he'll be back soon." David tried to sound optimistic.

"We don't really know that for certain, Mr Easton,"

the captain replied angrily before storming off to the bridge.

Diana approached David and gave him a playful punch in the arm. "Well done. That was quite a show. By the way, don't for a moment think that I didn't see you checking out your own tushie. Whistling while you were doing it was a nice touch."

"I was doing it in the name of science," he stated.

"I bet you were." She forced a smile. "So, what's plan B?"

David held up his plastic zip bag from the test kit. "I have no idea if I collected anything, but the sponge and test tubes have to be examined."

"Was there even anything to take a sample from? You never seemed to be fully inside of whatever it is."

"I'll know when I get these to the microscope."

"Are you planning on parading through the boat like that?" She glanced down at his flowery swimsuit.

He had completely forgotten to get dressed after getting out of the wetsuit. He stepped over to where his clothes had been carefully left for him and dressed quickly.

"Would you do me a favour and ask your father to join me in the infirmary?"

Diana looked back at him with a pained expression.

"What's wrong?" David was almost afraid to ask.

"He's gone. When he came back from the wireless tour he sat down and said that he must be getting old, as his feet had gone numb. We got his shoes off and it was already at his knees. It was very quick."

David took her in his arms.

"I am so very sorry. We both know he will be back, but to have watched both your parents be taken – I can't even imagine that."

She gently broke the embrace. "Can I help in the lab?"

"More than you'll ever know," he replied.

CHAPTER
EIGHTEEN

David tipped the two surgical sponges onto a Petri dish, then took the sealed test tubes and sat them in a wooden holder.

"Which are you going to try first?" Diana asked.

"I think the sponges should go first. If there is anything there, we don't want it to dry out." He put on a pair of rubber gloves and gently picked up one of the sponges. He pressed it hard against a sterile glass slide, then placed it immediately onto the microscope's stage.

He looked through the eyepiece. All he could see was the mild distortion from the glass itself. He increased magnification but still saw nothing. He repeated the same process with the second sponge, but with the same results.

"Nothing?" Diana asked.

"It was a long shot anyway. Let's try one of the test tubes. I was able to take the stopper off each for a few seconds. There must be a trace of something."

David located a bottle of isopropyl alcohol and carefully drew a small amount into a syringe. He injected two millilitres through the stopper and into the test tube. He then placed it in the small centrifuge. He loaded a balancing test tube in the opposing slot, replaced the cover and turned it on.

They both stared almost hypnotised, as the test tubes spun around at over 12,000 RPM.

After ten minutes he carefully removed the test tube and held it up to a light.

"Oh my god," David said as he stared at the bottom of the glass tube.

A wisp of green matter was clearly visible. Though liquid, it seemed to have no weight. David quickly dipped a pipette into the tube and withdrew the contents. He placed it on a slide, then onto the microscope.

He looked through the eyepiece.

"I've never seen anything like this. It's not even possible…"

Diana screamed.

David looked up and followed her glance. The test tube with the remains of the sample had grown black. Hairline cracks had begun to form. The pipette looked as if it had melted into an oily goo.

"Your gloves!" she cried.

The tips of his right-hand rubber glove looked to have calcified. And were visibly rotting in front of them. David shook both gloves off without even touching them.

He and Diana backed away from the testing table as they watched the microscope age before their eyes. It corroded, then rusted, then seemed to melt into a rust-coloured ooze. The table itself started to dissolve.

The entire room transformed into a rotted shell. Green mould covered the walls and ceilings until their shape was completely masked by sea grass and deep ocean molluscs. A pale white crab slowly moved across the mound that had been the microscope.

The pair backed into the passageway and watched with some relief as the destruction seemed to have stopped at the door.

"What the heck have you done to my infirmary?" Doctor Williams scolded them as he walked up behind them.

They turned to face him. He seemed to be smiling.

"I'm just pulling your leg. That testing area has never had such a workout. I'm pleased it's being used."

They looked at him with utter disbelief, then turned back to the room.

It was pristine. The only things out of place were the pair of rubber gloves on the floor and the slide that had been on the microscope stage. It was gone.

"Are you two all right? What did you see in there?"

They headed straight for Diana's suite. Partially to check if Arthur had returned but also so they could attack his private stock of brandy.

They were greeted by Myra the moment they entered the suite.

"He's back," she announced.

Something in her expression and tone seemed to lack some of the joy one would have expected.

"Sorry about my absence. How did the fog test go?" Arthur asked as he walked into the salon.

Diana turned to him with a relieved smile, then saw his face. There was no doubt Arthur had indeed returned, however there were some things about him that were simply wrong. Unlike the earlier people that had reanimated with only a patch or two of dead skin as a result, the process had radically changed for Arthur.

His right ear was the wrong size. It was too small and didn't match the other one at all. His eyes were much rounder than before his reanimation and their original blue colour had changed to a very dark purple. His mouth was substantially bigger than before and seemed to be stuck in a perpetual smile.

There were dozens of small differences. The biggest and most obvious one needed no close observation. His left arm was missing. Arthur looked like a copy of himself that was full of mistakes.

"I look a little odd, don't I?" he observed. "Believe it or not, I feel great. A little lopsided, but considering the alternative…"

"Oh Daddy!" Diana ran to him and threw her arms around her father. Arthur just managed to hug her with his remaining one.

David went to the small bar and poured three large brandies. Myra didn't need one. She seemed to have been doing a good job working diligently on a bottle of gin.

"You really feel okay?" David asked with concern.

"Fit as a fiddle," Arthur replied. He gave them all a big smile, presumably to ease their concerns. Unfortunately, because of his new mouth size and shape, the smile looked almost inhuman. It stretched too far across his cheeks causing his entire face to cringe upwards. It also permitted everyone to see that he clearly had a lot more teeth than before.

"Darling, I told you before – please don't smile like that," Myra slurred. "You look like a demented hyena."

Arthur turned to a gilt-framed mirror and studied his face for a moment. He then tried out his new expanded smile. He actually cringed and backed away from the reflective surface.

"Oh dear. That is a little alarming," he voiced.

They were interrupted by the telephone ringing.

Arthur went to answer it, but found he was unable to with a cocktail in one hand and his other no longer in existence.

David stepped over and answered it. He listened for a few seconds then hung up.

"The captain wants to see us immediately."

"Can't see the 'arm in that!" Myra joked drunkenly.

The captain was in his cabin, standing with his back to the small coal fire. He looked to have aged twenty years since they last saw him. He offered a forced smile for Diana and David then noticed the newly remodelled version of Arthur.

"Ah. I see you've just recently returned," he said. "It would appear that the reconstruction elves have been a bit remiss with their latest detail work."

There was a knock on the door.

"Come," Havelin shouted.

Commander Hess walked into the room. At least it seemed to be him. He was a full foot shorter than before, had lost most of his hair, had one ear missing and his nose was positioned three inches off centre. It sat almost directly under his right eye. His left eye was drooping and had turned an opaque milky colour.

He immediately noticed Arthur's condition.

"I feel like an incorrectly assembled Airfix model," Hess remarked in a slightly slurred voice.

"At least you returned with all the important parts." Arthur tried to make light of their situation.

The captain cleared his throat. "I asked you to join me here to find out if you discovered anything from the fog test? Things are deteriorating at an increased pace and we need some sort of an answer."

"As you witnessed on deck, it's not fog. It doesn't even seem to be elemental at all. It doesn't follow the laws of physics either. When I tried to examine a trace element from one of the test tubes it corrupted and destroyed the entire testing room," David advised.

"It destroyed the room? You mean it's gone?" Havelin asked.

"Actually, no. It returned to perfect condition again," Diana said.

"So, did you get a chance to examine the sample?"

"Actually, I did. It was just for a split second but that was enough time for me to see it," David replied.

"And?" Havelin pressed.

David looked to the others trying to decide whether to tell them the truth about what he had seen.

"As I said, I only saw it for a second," he paused. "I saw a flash of what I can only describe as a divine light, then I saw… infinity."

"David, what does that even mean? Infinity?" Arthur asked.

"I can't even begin to describe it. I've been trying to find the words since I first looked at the slide but with every minute that passes, my memory of what I saw seems to fade. I just remember thinking that I was looking at the very heart of existence. Then all hell broke loose."

"Was that when the room was destroyed?" the captain asked in a doubting voice.

"We both saw the lab turn into what looked like an undersea cave," Diana defended.

"We're hearing reports like that ship-wide," the captain advised. "When the lab returned to its normal form, were you able to check the slide again?"

"It was gone. Everything returned to the way it was except that the slide and the second test tube had vanished."

"That's a shame." Havelin sighed. "What do you make of the fog's new form?"

David, Diana and Arthur gave him a deer-in-the-headlights expression.

"Ah!" Havelin exclaimed. "You haven't observed the latest development? Please join me on the port bridge wing. I think you'll want to see this."

They followed the captain onto the bridge, then outside onto the suspended wing used for better visibility during docking manoeuvres.

"What do you see that's different?" he asked. Almost proudly.

They looked at the fog and couldn't make out any real change. It may have been a fraction greener but that was about it. They looked questioningly at the captain.

"Look up."

They did. Their expressions mirrored their utter shock.

The fog was no longer just a cloudy mass around the *Oceanis*. It now arched over the top of them. It looked almost solid. It curved over them like a canopy, from one side of the ship to the other. It swirled and eddied about thirty feet above the tops of the two funnels.

"That's most unusual," Arthur announced.

"It gets better," the captain said. "Watch this."

He pulled a brass lever attached to the bridge wing railing. The ship's horn blasted its moody cry.

The fog above them seemed to react to the sound. The swirling became almost frantic. Dark waves rippled across its surface. Then a brief downpour drenched them.

"You could have warned us." Diana's thin blouse had turned partially see-through.

"I wanted you to experience this as we did earlier," the captain replied. "Unprepared."

"But we're soaked," David said.

"Taste the water," Havelin requested.

The three tasted it.

"That's not possible," Arthur announced.

The captain just shrugged his shoulders.

"It's salty," Diana said.

"Of course it is, my dear. It's sea water," Havelin announced.

"We now have sea water above us?" David asked.

"So it would appear," the captain replied almost cheerfully.

CHAPTER
NINETEEN

Exhausted, yet happy to be all together, David joined Diana, Myra and Arthur for dinner in the Veranda Grill. Arthur had initially wanted to stay in their suite as he felt a little self-conscious about his new appearance and didn't want to be seen in public quite yet but Myra had told him to stop being so vain and to just get used to it. She felt that he was unlikely to be the only one in the restaurant with reanimation anomalies.

It turned out she was right. There were at least a dozen people who appeared to have undergone some exceptionally unorthodox re-design work. Arthur's oddities were, with the exception of the arm, subtle compared to some of the other diners.

An otherwise elegant woman at the next table had eyes that bulged so far out of the sockets, it looked as if someone had glued ping-pong balls on either side of her nose.

A poor man a few tables away looked like his face had melted onto his chest. His eyes were now where his chin had been and his mouth seemed to protrude from his sternum. Despite the facial deformities, the man was knocking back martinis between mouthfuls of beef wellington. Watching him shovel food into his chest was one of the strangest things they had ever witnessed, even considering what they had seen over the last few days. David just hoped that the man's internal plumbing was in line with the external work or things could get nasty.

However, by far the strangest aberration was that of a young girl that they'd all seen around the ship with her parents. She had looked startlingly similar to Shirley Temple when the actress was six years old.

That resemblance was now long gone. The child had been reanimated with the limbs of an adult. Not just from one person, either. Her left arm seemed to belong to an elderly woman. Her right, to a muscle-bound man. Both her legs seemed to be male. One was exceptionally long while the other was just shorter than average. Her beautiful young face was now half the size of the original, yet had the features of an obese woman. Her body was the only part that looked almost original. With the small head and the over-length limbs, she looked like a contented spider, as she worked diligently on a nut-covered chocolate sundae.

Her parents were chatting away to her as they gulped down their cocktails. They were doing their best to act as if nothing had happened, though their eyes held a dark pain that no amount of alcohol could ever fully conceal.

Myra had bullied her way into the restaurant seating her group at one of the most prized tables. They had an unobstructed view facing aft. From where they were, they could clearly see the stern docking bridge and the aft flag pole.

The deck lighting seemed to be refracting back from the fog canopy, adding an eerie green hue to everything. They tried to keep the mood as light as possible. Even Myra seemed oddly pleasant and was even accepting of David's presence.

They had just finished their main course and were deciding on desserts when Diana let out a tiny cry. Her parents were arguing about how to find a suitable replacement for his missing limb so hadn't heard her.

"What's wrong?" David moved his chair closer to her.

"It's my left foot," she whispered as a single tear ran down her cheek. "It feels like something's growing on it."

David unobtrusively glanced down to have a quick check.

"Does it feel almost like it's wrapped in something?"

She nodded.

David reached down and untangled her dinner napkin from her ankle.

They both stared down in stunned silence for a moment then started to howl with laughter. People from the other tables glared at them for finding amusement, considering the situation.

After dinner, Arthur and Myra retreated to their suite as David and Diana chose to have a stroll on Sun Deck. Though it was close to midnight, they were bathed in the eerie green light from the fog. It was even more intense than earlier as the crew had switched on a pair of klieg lights that were pointed directly up at the canopy. They found a couple of deckchairs and lay next to each other as they stared up at the new phenomenon.

"It's almost beautiful," Diana said.

"I would find it more beautiful if I knew what the hell it was."

"Don't spoil the moment," she chided.

"Yes, ma'am."

David reached over and took her left hand in his right. They lay there in complete silence.

"What the hell was that?" David asked as he stared at one particular spot in the canopy.

"Can't you just lie quietly… wait… I see it too." She pointed up at a dark shape moving within the mass above them. "What is that?"

They both watched the thing dart back and forth above them. It seemed to be the size of one of the lifeboats but its shape was hard to distinguish amid the constant motion of the grey-green canopy.

Then it came to the very edge of the fog. As it moved just within the grey-green mass, they could almost make out the shape. Then a single dorsal fin appeared. Even upside down, they both recognised what it was.

It was a shark, but not like any shark they had ever heard about. Its mouth was grotesquely out of proportion with its body. Its jaw held row after row of needle-like teeth. It was swimming within the canopy directly above their heads. One of the klieg lights caught the creature in its beam for a brief moment just as its head broke free of the surface. They both realised at the same time that the fog had changed. It was no longer fog-like at all.

They were looking up at what appeared to be clear green sea water.

They sat watching the bizarre display for over an hour. Other passengers and crew heard about the mysterious upside-down ocean show and had crowded the deck. Their necks were craned as they stared upwards. Every so often, something below the upside-down surface would agitate the liquid causing bucket-loads of sea water to splash down on the audience.

They seemed to love it.

Diana and David finally decided to call it a night. There was only so much upside-down ocean frolicking one could take in one evening.

David was concerned that Diana would want to return to her suite to be closer to her parents, considering what they'd both been through. He was wrong. Diana needed an escape from reality. David was delighted to learn that he had been chosen to be the critical player in her emotional escape plan.

There was nothing gentle or romantic about their lovemaking that night. It was primal. The fears and horrors that had filled their psyches found at least a temporary respite through raw lust. Neither seemed to be able to find satisfaction. The sex became even more desperate and frantic.

It was as if they realised that this could be the very last time they ever experience such pleasures again in this lifetime.

Finally, seemingly spent, the two lay in each other's arms. They didn't speak. They silently tried to make some sense of what they had recently seen and experienced.

Despite their exhaustion, Diana leant over and kissed David gently on the mouth. He softly kissed her back. Before they knew it, they were making love again, but this time there was a tenderness and ease that only comes from trust and deep affection.

As they both fell into a deep sleep, David again found himself in the same dream where he was lost within his old apartment building. This time, he found a door he didn't remember ever having seen before. He opened it and stepped through into the plush casino onboard the *Oceanis*.

He was greeted warmly by Captain Havelin and was shown to the only available seat at a blackjack table. A pile of chips appeared in front of him.

The players placed their bets on the table then the dealer dealt each player two cards face down. He then dealt himself two cards, one up, one down. He had a jack showing. David looked at his cards and saw that he had an ace and a queen. He felt a wave of relief. He had winning cards.

David turned to look at the other players and saw that he was suddenly the only one at the table. He scanned the room and realised that he was the only passenger in the entire place.

David looked over at the dealer and gasped. He had turned into one of the recently reanimated. Everything was wrong with him. He had one eye on his right cheek and a tiny mouth low down on the left side of his jaw. He had no ears or nose. His head was impossibly long and was attached to his body by a neck the width of a pencil.

The grotesque face smiled back at David.

The dealer turned over his cards. He had a pair of jacks. David proudly flipped his cards over. His perfect hand had turned into a pair of twos.

David felt panic. He looked to the bet he had placed on the green baize and saw that it was no longer there. He then realised that all of his chips were gone.

"You can't be in the game without being willing to lose, Mr Easton," Captain Havelin whispered from behind him.

The two thugs from engineering appeared on either side of him. They held him in his seat while the dealer reached across the table with a wizened grey arm and grabbed hold of David's right arm. The dealer began to physically turn David's hand. It started to unscrew from the wrist. David saw that it was threaded and amazingly seemed to rotate quite easily.

The hand came off and the dealer dropped it into a large metal bin on his left. David was just able to see into it from his position. It was full of body parts. He suddenly recognised that some of them were his.

He looked down and saw that both his legs were gone as was his left arm.

The dealer smiled with his tiny, repositioned mouth and dealt two more cards to David.

"You can't stop now, Mr Easton. You still have plenty to play for," Havelin whispered menacingly.

David shuddered awake and saw Diana curled up next to him. He lay there for hours, scared to fall asleep again. The dreams were becoming stranger and yet more real every time.

Despite his efforts at staying awake, sleep ultimately

crept up on him and took him back into its cold and unforgiving realm.

His only dream was of him frantically trying to swim to his table in the main dining room. He was battling a strong current and was making little headway. Diana was swimming next to him and seemed to be doing a far better job. She shouted for him to take hold of her waist so that she could pull him along. It worked. They were actually getting closer to their table.

The ship's emergency alarm system jolted them both awake. There were no announcements or warnings, just a wailing banshee-like alarm and strobing red lights.

They threw on their clothes and stepped out of David's cabin. They had expected to see chaos, yet the passageway was empty. People were all standing in their doorways curious to know the cause of the alarm and what they should do.

Andrew, the steward, appeared, running down the passageway.

"Don't be alarmed. It's just a small issue at the stern of the ship. You are in no danger."

He repeated the announcement a dozen times as he ran down each passageway on Main Deck.

David and Diana knew that there were no such things as small issues any more onboard the *Oceanis*. They felt they needed to check out just what had triggered a ship-wide alarm.

They made their way aft to the stern stairway and climbed up one flight. They decided that the best view without any crowds would be from the Veranda Grill.

They expected the place to be busy with breakfast service for the first-class suites but found themselves to be the only passengers in the restaurant.

They stood at the picture windows among the concerned restaurant staff and looked down at the aft deck. They couldn't see anything amiss, though there was quite a crowd on the fantail, all trying to look down at the stern. There didn't seem to be any panic, just curiosity.

"What's everyone looking at?" David shouted over the alarm.

"Apparently, there's a problem with the props," a steward yelled back.

The alarm suddenly stopped. The sudden silence was deafening.

"What sort of problem?" Diana asked.

"I heard that the prop shafts are befouled," the steward explained.

"What does that mean?" David asked.

"Not a clue, sir. But judging by the to-do, it can't be something good."

Diana noticed the captain standing on the aft bridge wing. He was looking directly up at them. He resumed staring over the side of the ship, then walked back into the aft wheelhouse.

They continued to look at the commotion below them. They really couldn't understand the fuss. There was nothing unusual to see at all. They continued gawking anyway.

"You'll not see anything of value from here," Captain Havelin announced from behind them.

His presence in the restaurant had sent the grill's staff scurrying back to their assigned duties.

"How's your knowledge on metallurgy?" he asked.

"It wasn't my major, but I can tell steel from aluminium."

"Good enough. Come with me."

The captain turned and started to walk away. He clearly expected them to follow closely behind.

"Sir?" David said. "Would you mind giving us some idea of where we're going and why?"

The captain stopped and slowly turned to face him.

"It appears that something is corroding the prop shafts and rudder housings."

"I would have thought that was a common problem on a ship," David replied.

"Not like this. This is not common in any way. We've lost one prop already and both the ship's rudders have gone."

David could only stare back at him. He had no idea what to say.

"It would be of great help if you could have a look at the problem and maybe, if possible, take a sample for examination. Will you please come with me?" the captain asked again.

"Yes, sir," they both immediately replied.

CHAPTER
TWENTY

They followed the captain through a labyrinth of passageways and staircases that David didn't even know existed. They ended up in the ship's aft engine room. It was vast. The massive turbines were each the size of a house. The first thing they noticed was the heat and the noise. It was beyond what one imagined as tolerable for a human being.

"How can anyone work in these conditions?" David had to shout to be heard.

"This is nothing. We're not running the engines at the moment. What you're hearing is just the ship's generators. If you think this is hot now, you should be down here when we're making steam for full flank speed."

He led them through a series of massive watertight bulkhead doors that ran between the two port engines. They arrived at one labelled SHAFT TUNNEL.

"This is where it gets interesting," Havelin announced.

They entered a gloomy space that had a raised, railed walkway on the right that ran over fifty feet to the stern of the ship. On the left was a giant cylindrical metal casing that also ran the length of the room. It looked like part of a sewer system.

"Is that the propeller shaft?" Diana asked.

"No, it's not. What you're looking at is the stern tube. The shaft is inside that," he explained. "There are two of these in total. One for each prop."

They walked halfway along the room then stepped down a small metal staircase so they could approach the shaft tube. Two crewmen were standing to attention next to an open examination panel. One of the men turned on a high-powered work light and held it over the opening to give the captain and his guests a better chance of seeing the inside of the tube.

The three stepped closer so they had a clear view inside the cylinder. The propeller shaft should have been a six-foot-diameter, well-lubricated, highly-polished steel rod within the external casing, however what they saw was a heavily corroded and rusted piece of metal that would never again be functional. The rust had eaten away huge chunks of the shaft. Cracks were visible everywhere. The once shiny rod was now a mottled greenish grey, with sections of orange rust showing through.

One of the crewmen led the group to the last examination panel before the shaft exited the hull and connected to one of the ship's twenty-foot-wide, eight-bladed brass propellers.

They looked into the opening. The propeller shaft ended in a rusted nub two feet before reaching the stuffing box that would have kept it watertight as it passed through the hull.

David was shocked yet fascinated.

"May I?" He pointed to a screwdriver on the crewman's belt. The man glanced at the captain who gave him a brief nod.

"Here you are, sir." He handed David the tool.

David reached through the opening and was about to scrape some rust from the destroyed shaft.

"You may want to ensure that your hand stays on the plastic end," the crewman advised.

David gave him a puzzled look but did as instructed. He held the plastic handle tightly as he tried to scrape off a piece of the corrosion. He couldn't seem to get a purchase against the shaft. He then realised that the screwdriver was bending at the end. He withdrew it and saw that the metal of the driver had started to corrode and rust as he watched.

"You'd best just toss it into the tube," Captain Havelin suggested.

David dropped it immediately.

"Thoughts?" the captain asked.

"My first thought is that I won't be getting any samples."

"Understood," Havelin conceded.

"How long has it been like this?" David's voice broke.

"Let's put it this way. When I went up to check out the stern rudder connectors, the shaft was still intact and passed through the stuffing box."

"Are you saying this happened today?" Diana couldn't keep the panic from her voice.

"I'm saying it happened within the last two hours. Both shafts are the same. The ship's rudders came off about an hour ago."

"The rudders came off?" David gasped. "Please tell me that that's a nautical term for being out of alignment or something."

"No. That's a term for when a pair of 250-ton rudders fall off the bloody ship," Havelin growled.

"Has whatever's been rotting the metal stopped now?" Diana asked, hoping for some good news.

"Far from it. The corrosion has started eating away at the stern hull plating. It's almost as if it's planning to devour the entire ship."

She wished she hadn't asked.

As they stood looking down at the ruined shaft, David noticed something just above the stuffing box. The painted inner section of the double metal hull had started to blister. They watched in real time as the blisters grew then cracked. Within seconds, liquid rust ran down the steel plate from each one.

They backed away while keeping their eyes locked on the spreading rusticles. The ship's iron was deteriorating at an inexplicable speed.

"Why is this happening, Mr Easton?" the captain asked.

"I wish I knew, sir. What we are looking at is not physically possible. The iron is going through a process that should take years if not decades. And even then, the metal would have to be submersed in water the entire time."

"But we are in water," Diana pointed out.

"The outer hull is in contact with water. The inner hull most definitely is not, or at least shouldn't be," the captain replied.

The corrosion had spread to the surrounding steel plates. The earlier affected ones were no longer rust coloured. They had turned to a powdery green even as new rusticles seemed to form on their surface.

"Are we going to sink?" Diana asked.

"Looking at the damage we've sustained already, we should be standing in three feet of sea water already," Havelin explained. "The integrity of the stuffing boxes, the rudder mounting plates and now the hull plates have gone far beyond their capability to remain watertight. There's no good reason why we haven't seen breaches throughout the below water areas of the stern."

"Is it only affecting metal?" David asked as they watched a crewman replace the furthest aft inspection plate. As he was fastening the final bolt, a tiny rusticle ran down the side of the tube and dropped onto his hand.

He tried to brush it off but his hand almost immediately turned a mottled green. Flesh started to fall off the bones. The man's clothing began to rot at an horrific speed. His flesh shrivelled then fell off his skeleton in lumps that dissolved into water as they hit the floor. His skeleton then collapsed onto the metal decking and it too dissolved. The only thing that remained was a brass nameplate that was corroding at an impossible speed.

"I'd say it's affecting way more than just metal," Havelin exclaimed. "We need to get topside – now!"

The three were joined by the second seaman as they made their way out of shaft alley.

Diana and David headed straight for the Olsons' suite to warn her parents. They were relieved to find both Myra and Arthur sitting comfortably in the dining area enjoying breakfast.

"We were wondering if you'd be joining us," Arthur said. "We ordered enough for a small army."

"Try the smoked salmon and eggs," Myra insisted. "They really are quite delicious."

"They most certainly are." Arthur gave them one of his new, creepy, oversized smiles.

They realised that despite what they had just been through, they were actually hungry. They also shared the same concern of not knowing when they would next be able to eat. Though if the crew couldn't get a handle on that corrosion, a lack of food would be the least of their problems.

They sat and tucked into the breakfast feast. Arthur hadn't been kidding. Apart from the eggs and smoked salmon, there were fresh bagels, assorted pastries, bacon and grapefruit.

When Myra left the table to 'freshen up' Arthur turned to face them.

"You both looked to be in complete shock when you walked in here. What's happened? Was it something to do with that alarm earlier?"

They quickly gave him the rundown of what they'd seen in the shaft tunnel. He listened closely, nodding his head occasionally.

"We will need to keep an eye on that," Arthur announced once he'd heard the entire saga. "That could end up being a problem."

"The propellers and rudder have fallen off the ship," David whispered. "I think it already qualifies as a problem."

"Not necessarily," Arthur replied. "It's not as if we have been going anywhere, have we? My concern is more about the rot taking over the entire ship. Then again…" He stopped to pop an entire bran muffin into his extra-large mouth. "I think that the ship is in good hands."

"I agree, but the captain doesn't have any idea what's going on either. And he definitely doesn't seem to know how to stop it."

"My dear boy, I wasn't referring to the captain. We haven't been under his governance for some time now. You must have seen that. Whatever it is that's guiding us now – I feel confident that it will get us to where we're meant to be."

As Arthur poured himself another coffee, David shot Diana a quick glance to check her reaction to her father's words.

She stared back at him, wide-eyed and scared.

"I mean, look at me. It's taken my life once already but brought me back even better than I was before."

Arthur produced the biggest smile yet. He seemed to have even more teeth than earlier. They were no longer white. They had yellowed and had patches of green moss growing between them.

"I think I need some air," Diana announced as she pushed her chair from the table.

"I'll join you." David practically jumped to his feet.

As they were leaving, Diana looked back at him. "Will we see you later?"

"That's not really up for me to say, is it?" he grinned just before devouring a prune Danish.

CHAPTER
TWENTY-ONE

The first thing they noticed when they reached Sun Deck was that it was still dark. As it was well past nine in the morning, they took that as a bad sign. They looked up at the ocean canopy. Without the klieg lights, it appeared to just be a dark mass that had completely encircled the ship.

A streak of luminescence shot across the dark liquid from port to starboard. Then another dim light passed gracefully over their heads. David was baffled.

"It's bioluminescence," Diana explained. "Judging by the light intensity, it's probably from fish."

"I've never seen fish that can light up like that."

"You wouldn't," Diana explained. "They only live in the Abyssopelagic layer of the ocean."

"This is a whole new side of you!" David looked surprised.

"It might be new to you but I've had that side for over twelve years. I summer interned at the Manhattan

Aquarium. I sat through more lectures than you could ever imagine."

"I never knew you were even interested in fish, except maybe on a plate," David joked.

"I wasn't. Daddy got me the job to keep me out from under his feet during one particular summer. I can't begin to tell you how much I hated him for that. I was planning on being a Hampton's beach bum. Turned out though that I loved the aquarium. Every day was fascinating. I even considered changing my major."

"To what – fish?"

She playfully punched his arm. "No, you dingbat! To marine biology."

"Why didn't you?" David asked.

"Too much science. I loved the whole concept but the science part was way out of my league. I seem to be a right brainer. I'm told I have a strong artistic leaning. Maths and science might as well have been taught in Chinese."

David's smile started to erode.

"What was that layer you mentioned? Abbyploddering or something?"

"The Abyssopelagic layer," she said.

"I hope that's the top layer of the ocean?"

"Far from it. It's almost the deepest layer. It gets zero sunlight so it's perpetually black down there. That's why the fish have adapted to be able to provide their own lighting."

"In that case, why is the deepest…"

"Second deepest," she corrected.

"Why is the second deepest layer of the ocean now above us?" David asked with forced calm.

"My feeling is that any ocean sitting above us is an aberration of nature. At this point, its depth is inconsequential," she added.

They continued their walk as they made for the stern to see if there had been any further corrosion noticeable from their deck.

There was a good number of passengers strolling on the deck. They didn't seem to be the least bit fazed by the fog's transition to sea water. The most disturbing thing was the number of passengers that seemed to have reanimated with grotesque abnormalities.

Over half were so extreme that it seemed impossible for them to survive at all, yet none seemed to even be aware of their conditions. They chatted away, they laughed. It was a picture of shipboard normalcy, yet of course, it really wasn't normal at all.

"Will you still love me if my face and butt change positions?" Diana asked deadpanned.

"You talk so much crap sometimes, I thought the process had already started," he volleyed back.

"You pig!" she scolded playfully.

As they reached the stern railing, they could hear the sound of metal crunching against metal. The crowd at the stern was three deep. They managed to find a place behind an unnaturally short couple. They tried not to dwell on the fact that they didn't look like they had always been of diminutive stature. Their torsos were almost obese. That part looked original. Their legs and arms looked to have come from very young children. Though their heads seemed to be the normal size, their faces looked almost mummified with age.

It was the first redesigned couple that appeared to have been reanimated with matching physical abnormalities. David couldn't decide if that was a blessing or curse.

For him and Diana it was a blessing. They had a perfect view over the top of them. Then again, once they'd seen what was happening, they wondered if ignorance of the situation wouldn't have been a better option.

The fantail of the *Oceanis* was being consumed by the green corrosion. The bioluminescence from above was so intense that the entire stern area was illuminated with pale green light that seemed to almost strobe with each new attack on the ship's structure.

The stern railing and the last five feet of the decking had already been decimated. Teak planks, freshly blackened by the rot, jutted into the air as they splintered under the pressure of the metal sub-decking contorting as it was being eaten away.

The second-class swimming pool had started to crack and shatter, sending shattered blue tile squares flying in all directions. David and Diana decided they had seen enough after they watched an ornate stainless-steel swim ladder shrivel and bend into an unrecognisable lump as it was consumed by the corrosive mass.

"It's going to destroy the entire ship, isn't it?" Diana asked.

"It looks that way."

"But what is it?"

David turned to her. "I know this sounds crazy, but it looks like the ship is ageing. That corrosion that we're seeing is exactly what would happen to a submerged ship but it should take years, even decades. This is happening in minutes."

"But it's not just ageing, is it? It's way more destructive than that. It's more like the ship's being turned into a wreck," she said.

"A shipwreck? That doesn't make sense. We're afloat. We're not sinking. A shipwreck doesn't start by rotting, then sinking. It's the other way around," David insisted.

"Whatever the sequence, the *Oceanis* is being systematically destroyed from the stern forward. If the damage can't be stopped, we need to find a way to get off this ship."

"How?" David asked. "The wireless radios are useless. The ship's communications aren't going anywhere."

"Let's go and talk to my father. Maybe between us we can come up with some idea. What if there's one lifeboat that's still intact. We could at least get away from this ship."

David walked up to the nearest lifeboat and studied it. It looked as solid as the day it was built. The davit mechanisms were useless but there could possibly be a way to lever the boat over the side from its current position.

He wrapped his knuckles against its wooden hull expecting to hear the sound of solid oak. His hand sank right into the boat's side. The wood had turned to mush. It seemed that the only thing that was keeping it intact was the heavy-duty nautical paint.

"That went well," Diana remarked.

As they headed back towards the bow they heard the distinct sound of a shotgun followed by wild cheering coming from the other side of funnel one's deck housing.

They made their way to the starboard side and stopped while they were still sheltered behind the superstructure. They carefully crept to the side of the housing just as another gun blast sounded and was again followed by cheering.

They eased their heads around the corner.

A queue of about thirty people were lined up in an orderly fashion. They all seemed extraordinarily excited. At the head of the queue, the deck steward who had been in charge of the clay-pigeon shooting, cradled a shotgun on his arm.

The next person in line stepped forward and stood in front of a large, painted wooden cut-out depicting a tropical paradise. Diana and David recognised it from the captain's welcome aboard party on the first night. Guests lined up to have their picture taken with the captain in front of the decorative standee.

As they looked on at the macabre re-enactment, they saw that the people weren't having their photo taken and the standee was covered in pellet holes.

The next passenger was in her fifties and was wearing a bright red ball gown. She seemed almost giddy. She stepped in front of the standee then adopted a hula dancer pose. She smiled at the steward as he raised the shotgun and let go with both barrels.

The woman disappeared in a big green puff. It reminded David of when he used to blow the dry head off a dandelion flower and would watch it disperse into the air.

A second steward stepped forward and efficiently removed the clothing that had dropped to the deck when the passenger evaporated.

The other passengers cheered as the next person in line began to move towards the paradise backdrop.

David took Diana's hand and, without a word, led her back to the port side of the ship. They found the nearest stairway and headed down.

The moment they entered the suite they could see that reality had taken another jump outside of the norm.

Arthur and Myra were standing at one of the salon windows. Though it was completely tarnished and offered zero visibility, they stood holding hands as they gazed out at nothing.

"We need to find a way off this ship. The blight is already destroying the stern. I'm not sure how long we have," David said.

"We're ready to go back, David." Arthur's voice sounded hollow.

"Go back to where? We've got to leave the ship immediately."

"We did everything we could," Arthur continued. "We were given a chance. Now it's time to go back."

"Daddy, what are you talking about?" Diana sounded scared. "You've got to listen to David. We need to do something. The passengers are acting crazy. I don't think we have long."

Her parents turned away from the window.

Diana screamed.

Her mother and father were slowly melting. The plush carpet they were standing on was already wet. Their bodies and clothes seemed to be turning into clear water that was flowing freely onto the floor.

Their features had softened. The edges had blurred as the liquid replaced flesh. It looked as if they were smiling but their mouths dissolved and ran down their chests.

"We love you, darling," Arthur said.

"We will always love you, sweetheart," Myra added.

Their words were becoming garbled as their vocal chords turned to liquid.

Arthur tried to say something else but all they could hear was a wet gurgling sound.

The process seemed to accelerate. The couple began to shrink in size as the puddle on the floor expanded. They no longer had any features as such. Their bodies were shapeless artefacts that quickly liquefied and pooled into the deep pile.

Diana and David saw that the furnishings within the room were starting to rot.

They backed out of the suite then ran as fast as they could till they deemed they were far enough from danger. At least that particular danger.

David held her close. She wasn't crying. She had already wept once after her parents' first deaths. She had somehow always known that there would be another, though not one like they had just witnessed.

"What now?" She looked up into his eyes.

"I think we should try to warn everyone to stay away from the stern. If people are still standing around watching the blight happen, they're gonna die," David suggested.

"What about the shooting?"

"We'll stay well clear of that. We'll go up the main staircase. That will put us well aft of that lunacy."

They made their way back up to Sun Deck and found that only a small handful of people was still observing the ship's seeming self-destruction. It had already consumed the entire fantail and was moving slowly forward, ravaging all decks at the same time.

They stood for a moment and watched with a twinge of sadness as it reached the Veranda Grill. The windows blew out and the roof began to crumble into the restaurant.

That was enough. They worked their way down the aft stairwell to the rear entrance of the main dining salon.

The room was unusually dark. What little light there was came from a single candle on each table. David's first reaction was one of relief. There seemed to be a semblance of normality. Then as his eyes adjusted to the dim lighting, he realised just how wrong he'd been.

The salon was full of diners and stewards yet there was no food or drink. Over 500 passengers were miming eating and drinking while the crew carried out the pretence of serving. What made the scene truly terrifying was that the pantomime was happening in complete silence. The diners looked to be carrying on conversations and even laughing, but there was no sound.

For a brief moment, the salon's lights all flickered to life, illuminating the giant room in its normal elegant fashion.

David and Diana could then clearly see that none of the people had faces. Just smooth, featureless flesh.

Diana caught her breath.

Every single sightless face turned to stare at them.

The lights flickered a few times then went off again. The diners and stewards turned away and resumed their previous dining parody.

Diana and David walked through the room as quietly and unobtrusively as possible. They considered finding another way forward but traversing the dining room saved a lot of time. They reached the dining room lobby and stopped. They looked to each other for some supportive reaction. They couldn't yet find the words to express the whirlpool of impossible thoughts that were circling within their minds.

They kept moving and reached the central staircase lobby and were about to head up and forward when they heard laughter. Lots of it. It sounded like a large group of people actually having fun.

They followed the sounds of mirth and arrived at the ship's full-sized cinema. They walked into the foyer and found the popcorn and drinks counter in full operation. People were loading up with as much as they could carry. The laughter bled through from the auditorium. It was beyond raucous.

Diana took David's hand as she led him cautiously to the stairs leading up to the balcony. He realised that she didn't feel safe walking straight into whatever was going on beyond the main auditorium doors.

They carefully opened one of the double doors leading to the balcony seats. Her instincts had been right. There was nobody there at all. The audience was all seated below in the main auditorium. They walked forward to the balcony railing.

The sound of the laughter was almost deafening. The cinema lights were low but they could see well enough. Every seat below was full. People were howling with laughter. Children were laughing so hard they had tears running down their faces. When heard up close, the gleeful sounds seemed strangely insincere, even forced.

People's faces were red and strained at the effort to sustain so much false joy and happiness.

Between laughs they were filling their mouths with handful after handful of popcorn. This was interspersed with messy gulps of soda. None of it seemed to actually get swallowed, yet the feeding frenzy never abated for a second, except when a new roar of pseudo laughter again captured the audience.

Even though the auditorium was dimly lit, David and Diana had no trouble seeing that the cinema screen's curtains were closed and the screen was not visible. That wasn't really surprising considering that nothing was being projected anyway.

They glanced at each other for a brief second then started to exit the balcony.

The double doors flew open and an usher rushed in towards them. He was carrying a giant tub of popcorn in one hand and balancing two large sodas in the other.

"You two should be downstairs," the young man advised. "The picture and sound is much better down there."

He forced the drinks and popcorn into David's and Diana's arms.

"Stay up here if you like, but when the movie is over, we'll be having a trivia quiz. You have to be downstairs for that."

He scurried out of the double doors leaving them alone on the balcony.

They looked down at the popcorn and soda cradled in their arms. The popcorn was grey and was covered in black mould. The soda was dark yellow and had a film of oily discharge floating on top.

They placed their loot carefully on the floor then snuck out of the balcony just as another raucous wave of hysterical laughter rocked the auditorium.

They made their way back to the central stairwell lobby and just stood there, not knowing where to go at that point.

"What's happening?" Diana asked.

"I'd say that reality as we know it is starting to unravel."

"What the hell does that mean?"

"It means that we are on our own," David replied. "We should head towards the bow if we want to have any chance of surviving this."

"There is no surviving this, is there?" Diana replied. She sounding exhausted and despondent.

"Don't give up now," David urged. "We just have to keep moving."

"Why? Haven't you seen what's going on? Whatever all this is—" She gestured theatrically with her hands. "It's obviously coming apart at the seams."

"Not for us," he shouted. "I won't let it happen to us."

"How the hell are you going to stop it? It's everywhere. It's insane."

"Exactly!" he insisted. "None of this can be real. It's all an illusion."

She turned to face him head on. "In that case, please make it stop. I can't take any more of this."

"Yes, you can. You're stronger than you think. The important thing is to not give up. We have to just keep moving."

"Promise me that you will tell me when it's considered good manners to start screaming my damn head off, won't you?" Diana asked. "Somehow they left that part out of the curriculum at my finishing school."

"You'll know when it's time. I'm pretty sure I'll have started screaming long before you," he replied.

"That's reassuring." She managed to force a smile.

They left the lobby and entered a passageway that seemed to run the entire length of the ship. David glanced back aft.

He froze.

"I think we'd better get a move on." David's attention was focused on the far end of the hallway. The end closest to the stern.

Diana followed his gaze and saw that at the aft end, the passageway was dark. There was just enough ambient light however, to observe that the wood-panelled hallway was now a rotted shell. They could see right through the sides of the ship to the wall of water beyond. It hadn't yet encroached into the ship. It was just there.

Waiting.

The blight was moving slowly down the hall towards them. The overhead lighting dimmed and flickered just as the decay reached and destroyed each overhead crystal light fixture, one at a time.

"I don't remember seeing pictures like that in the *Oceanis* brochure!" she quipped nervously.

"I have an idea," David announced.

He grabbed her hand and practically dragged her up the stairway.

"Where are we going?" she asked.

"I don't know about you, but I am not ready to just keep running. I want to try something."

"It better be good. Otherwise I'm going back to see the rest of that movie. It looked like a hoot."

CHAPTER
TWENTY-TWO

David retraced his steps from the day before and found the door to the wireless communication centre. It was on Sun Deck inside the deck house that framed the base of funnel number one. They could see that the blight had already reached the second funnel which thankfully was a few hundred feet further aft. Its normally cheerful blue colour had been replaced with sea growth and rust. It had also started to lean precariously to starboard having lost its lower support structure to the corrosive rot.

"Whatever you plan to do, you'd better make it quick," Diana shouted.

David opened the door to the wireless room and was relieved to find that there were no operators at their work stations. He then stepped next door and walked into the equipment room. Diana looked about the space in amazement.

"Do you actually have any idea what this stuff does?"

"Some of it. The principle is pretty straightforward. Sound is changed into electric energy waves, then they are transmitted to receivers, at which point amplifiers feed them to speakers that convert them back to sound," he explained.

"That's what you call straightforward?" she joked.

He shrugged then spent the next few minutes tracing cables to and from various devices. Once he was able to work out the exact signal path, he started rewiring certain units. He ran a number of cables from one of the new-looking black booster boxes and reconnected them to a distribution amplifier. That done, he began adjusting dials on a number of pieces of equipment.

"I hope you know what you're doing," Diana voiced.

"So do I," he replied. "Basically, I am trying to boost the power to the old telegraph sender. That's the thing they used to use to send a Morse code signal."

"That, I've heard of," she grinned.

"I'm going to try using this new booster to amplify the signal we're going to send out. We know that the regular wireless signals are being blocked. My hope is that the Morse code signal will be so insignificant that it might just pass through the blockage but by boosting it, it should hopefully have a greater range."

"Have you ever done anything like this before?" Diana asked.

"I'm not sure anyone has," he replied.

"Well, that's a relief then."

As he continued to adjust the various pieces of equipment, they heard a deafening metallic squeal then the entire room shook. The overhead lights started to flicker.

Diana ran to the short hallway and stuck her head out of the door. She looked aft and saw that the second funnel had collapsed. The decking around the housing had already been consumed by the blight. The rot was making its way towards the base of the funnel that they were working under. She could see it wouldn't take long for it to cover the hundred or so feet to reach where they were standing. She ran back to David.

"Funnel number two's gone," she advised him.

"I'm done. Let's give it a go."

They went next door to the radio room. David stationed himself at the telegraph key and sounder. He switched on a small speaker then tapped the key a few times. There was dead silence. He tried again. Still nothing. He began tracing the various wires on the desk.

Diana looked under the desk.

"Is that pluggy thing supposed to be attached?" she asked.

He looked under the desk and clucked loudly.

He plugged the unit into a wall socket then tried the key again.

The sound of an electric beep came out of the speaker.

He looked to Diana and gave her a brave smile.

"Here we go." He began the sequence, '... – – – ...'

He repeatedly tapped out the international code for SOS. Three dots, three dashes, three dots. Diana was looking at a small Bakelite box just to the right of the sender. It had the words KEY REPEATER stamped on it.

"What's this do?"

David glanced at it and began to smile. He flipped the box's switch to the ON position.

He tapped the three dots, three dashes, three dots one more time on the sender then stopped. Nothing happened for a moment, then the sending key started tapping the signal by itself. They watched as it kept repeating the code.

"How long will it keep doing that?" Diana asked.

"Probably until someone turns it off," he suggested.

"Or something else stops it," Diana added.

The room shook violently and the lights flickered even more frantically. The little repeater, however, kept going.

They eased out of the door and when they looked up to the sports deck they saw with dread that the funnel had started to collapse inwards. As they watched in stunned horror, it suddenly folded in on itself with a deafening scream of rending steel. From their perspective the massive ship's funnel simply disappeared right down through the centre of the deck housing. The deck house itself had been spared but the blight was approaching fast.

"We'd better keep moving forward," David advised.

Diana nodded and took his hand.

They ran as far forward as they could on that deck. They climbed a crew-only metal staircase and emerged next to the bridge.

They opened a watertight door and stepped in. Captain Havelin and Commander Hess were the only two on the bridge. Hess was at the wheel. Havelin was standing, arms behind his back, as he looked forward into the artificial darkness through the bridge's storm-glass windows.

"Keep her at that heading," the captain ordered. "She's handling the waves well."

"Yes, Captain," Hess acknowledged.

"What a beautiful day," Havelin declared. "Couldn't have asked for better weather for this crossing."

David and Diana glanced up through the bridge windows and saw that they were still enveloped by the canopy of sea water.

"Captain?" David called out. "What's going on?"

The captain ignored him.

David approached him.

"Captain?" David touched the other man's arm. His hand went right through him. He seemed to be formed entirely from liquid. Havelin didn't react to the touch.

"Jesus Christ!"

Diana walked over to Hess and did the same thing. When she passed her hand through him, he seemed to shimmer for a moment then returned to appearing completely real.

Horrified, they backed out of the bridge and ran down the crew stairwell till they reached the watertight door that led to the foredeck.

They stepped out onto the deck and made their way forward to the bow. They were halfway there when the port anchor chain was torn from its massive winch and plunged, unrestrained, through the chain tunnel releasing the unseen anchor. The massive chain links began tearing through the teak decks until the weight of the anchor won out and severed one of the links.

They stood in shocked silence as they saw that the blight had now started consuming the bow and was moving aft. The sounds of the mighty ship being torn apart from all sides was beyond imagination. Wood, glass, metal – all had their own distinctive sound within the ship's dying melody. They watched as the destruction continued unabated.

Diana wiped a tear from her cheek.

"I know where I want to be," David shouted over the noise.

He grabbed her hand and pulled her back through the doorway and to the stairwell. Then ran down one flight of stairs and emerged into the forward staircase lobby. They walked through the Lalique doors and entered the ship's elegant Neptune Cocktail Lounge.

They were alone in the bar. It almost looked as if it had been spared any of the chaos that reigned just beyond its doors. There were some broken glasses and bottles that had been shaken loose when the funnel collapsed but other than that, it looked almost normal.

David went behind the huge bar and found two surviving brandy snifters. He filled both from a bottle of what looked to be highly unaffordable Napoleon VSOP brandy.

They walked to the floor-to-ceiling windows built within the ship's superstructure and looked down at the foredeck.

The decking was almost completely gone. The cargo hut and loading boom had fallen through to the cargo hold below. As they watched, the massive starboard anchor chain snapped sending it plummeting down into the void.

They could see in real time as the entire front of the ship decomposed and was then consumed by rust and sea growth.

A loud shattering sound caused them to turn just in time to see the bar's sixty-foot mirror shatter, sending a sparkling plume of silver and glass pieces onto the lounge floor. As they landed they immediately turned to shimmering liquid. The wall behind where the mirror had been affixed, started to decay. The walnut bar darkened to near black as it decomposed. The granite top began cracking, sounding like an ice flow tearing itself apart. The supporting wood then crumbled like cigar ash onto the floor.

The lights then went out for the last time.

Diana and David looked through the windows into the darkness. There was just enough light from the bioluminescence to see that the walls and canopy of ocean water were closing in on the ship.

The glass in the windows began to run onto the floor like water. The two suddenly found themselves looking outwards without any barrier between them and the encroaching elements.

David was about to speak when an extraordinarily bright light appeared from just above where the foredeck had been.

They had no idea what it was or what could cause such an extreme illumination. They both began to wave frantically just as the blight and the cocooning mass of ocean water reached them and entombed the final piece of the majestic liner.

CHAPTER
TWENTY-THREE

NOAA's research vessel *Columbus II* was being pummelled by the strong waves. It was built to withstand such treatment but the pounding still made it pretty uncomfortable for the ship's crew.

They were fighting to raise the manned submersible onto the aft deck cradle as the ship heeled violently from one side to the other. This had been their second dive that day trying to recover a damaged ocean-bed sensor.

The sensor had recorded a magnitude 8.1 earthquake forty-eight hours earlier, exactly at the point where the Eurasian and North American tectonic plates met. Then it had begun flashing error signals. Neither the folks at NOAA nor those on board were able to communicate with sensor forty-seven.

The force of the subduction had given the sea floor a good shaking. A number of fibre-optic data lines had been damaged and raised wave heights had been measured across the globe.

None of that mattered to Captain Morris and his crew. Their mission was to repair or replace the sensor unit.

Morris flipped his fifth cigarette of the day off the bridge wing. He'd just turned fifty and wasn't happy about it. Despite the smoking, he considered himself to be as fit as when he was back at the academy. Morris was convinced that there was something wrong with the bathroom mirror each time he saw the older face looking back at him.

He also didn't like being in the middle of the Atlantic with a nor'easter expected within forty-eight hours. He knew the $CO2$, as they referred to the ship, could outrun anything. He just wanted the work completed first.

On the second dive, the sub crew had managed to connect to the sensor unit and run diagnostics but found that the power supply unit had been damaged by something hitting it during the quake. One side of the sensor had been almost flattened.

They had no choice but to bring it to the surface and have the engineering team get a look at it. That meant that they were stuck out there for at least another full day. It was cutting it a little close.

Morris reached for another cigarette then decided that five was probably enough considering he'd given up ten days earlier.

"Cap?" His communications officer's voice filled his headset.

"What is it, Genna?" he replied through the voice-activated mic.

"You're not going to like this but another sensor in this sector just went bad. Can you come and have a look?"

She was right. Morris wasn't at all happy with that piece of news. He knew they'd have to check it out before running from the impending storm. The cost to leave it then return once the weather passed would be double if not more. He hated running a ship against a budget sheet.

"Sure. I'm on my way."

Morris passed through the bridge and down a half flight of metal steps. He entered a narrow passageway and walked through a full-height bulkhead doorway. The communications operations centre, or COC as the crew referred to it, was crammed full of every receiving and sending device imaginable. They had 24/7 access to military satellites, giving them constant sat phone access and T-1 quality bandwidth. They were able to communicate with anyone, anywhere.

The ship also had enough computing power to run a small country.

The captain switched his communications headset to manual mode.

"What ya got?" Morris asked as he squeezed into the cramped space.

Genna Washington was in her early twenties. Her ebony skin and bright red afro somehow suited her devil-may-care approach to life. She pointed to a ninety-inch touch screen. Dozens of green circles were scattered across a 4K rendering of the entire mid-Atlantic Ocean floor. Two of the circles were red and had black diagonal lines blinking within their icons.

"Forty-seven is on board for the geeks to fix, but number seventy-two just went down."

He approached the screen.

"Did you run diagnostics?" he asked.

She gave him a snarky expression. "Of course. There's no data exchange whatsoever."

He touched the flashing red circle on the flat screen. A pop-up appeared next to it. There were eighteen different system functions listed. All of them were in red.

"That's not possible. You can't lose all the systems at once and still have it sending out its ident and location. Can you?"

"The data feed and the ident are on two different transmitters in the sensor. Theoretically you could lose data and still keep getting the location ping," Genna said.

"Has that ever happened?" he asked.

"Nothing has ever happened until the first time it happens," she stated.

The captain rolled his eyes.

"That's one of the new units, right?"

"Yup. Got dropped six months ago," Genna replied.

"So, there's been no eyeball visit yet?" he asked.

"Hasn't been a need. Guess there is now. I'm sure it has something to do with the quake."

"Will you send the coordinates up to Brian. We are going to have to check it out before we try to outrun the weather. Let OPSCOM know that we've got a second sensor that's gone dark. Tell 'em we'll check it out and advise."

"I already spoke to Morgan at OPSCOM to get a verification. He seemed really happy that these failures were legit."

Morris gave her a puzzled look.

"He's the guy who had the fleet looking for a sensor that got picked up by a cable repair ship."

"I remember that fiasco. Poor guy. Wasn't really his fault." The captain laughed.

They reached the drop zone for sensor seventy-two in just under two hours. The seas were growing and the sky was starting to get interesting. It had turned dark purple with a greenish tinge on the horizon.

They got the submersible and its crew of two in the water as fast as was safe. They were able to track the sensor's emergency identifier and location beacon with no problem. The design was similar to those on board commercial aircraft, except ten times as powerful and with a five-year battery life.

Craig and Kendall Davis, NOAA's only husband and wife submersible crew, were in control of the tiny sub that was unfortunately named *Sad Eyes* as the result of some senator's hair-brained public naming competition.

To be fair, the twin slanted LED lights on the craft's nose plus the curved front skids, did make it look a little like a sad puppy.

It took almost two hours for the sub to reach the seabed. It was one of NOAA's deepest sensor locations at just over 25,000 feet.

Sunlight never reached that far down. The crew had to use all of the little sub's external lights to see anything. The descent was fully automated, but once they reached the sensor location, operating the external grabbers was a hands-on operation.

They reached the location where the emergency beacon should have been according to the tracking software, but saw nothing. They crept along only a few feet above the ocean floor as they scanned every inch of the barren seascape. The computer showed them being right on top of the sensor.

"Holy crap!" Kendall suddenly exclaimed.

Through the transparent nose of the sub, they could see that they were sitting right above a massive fissure. It was clearly new and must have been caused by the recent quake.

It was only about twelve feet wide but it seemed to be both deep and long. Their onboard laser mapping unit showed the crack continuing well beyond its ten-mile range.

"Surface – we don't think we are going to be able to retrieve this sensor," Craig advised.

"Copy that. Care to give us a reason?" The captain's voice came back loud and clear.

"We're on top of what looks to be a brand-new fissure. We can't see the sensor, but the locator shows it at 120 feet right below us. As we're in neutral five feet above the deck, we have to assume that it's fallen in," Colin said.

"Can you do a nose stand with full beams? Record everything so we can show the folks back home that we weren't just being lazy and gave up," Morris requested.

"Roger that," Kendall replied.

She took *Sad Eyes* a little higher off the seabed, then rotated the sub so it was pointed nose down, looking straight into the crack in the earth.

Kendall hit the full beams and the sad eyes lit up like a flash grenade. You couldn't keep them on full beam for long stretches or you'd drain the batteries but they were great for when you needed short bursts of mega light.

The front-facing video camera began recording.

On the surface ship, the ops crew together with Captain Morris had to suffice with low-res still pictures because of the depth. It was grainy and soft but they could see enough to know that if sensor number seventy-two was down there somewhere, there was no way to retrieve it even if they could see it.

"Captain?" Genna came through the com. "Could you come to the com centre, please?"

"Everything okay?"

"Not really, sir."

"I'll be right there." He again headed down the narrow hall.

He stepped into the com room and immediately heard a beeping sound that was barely audible above hissing and grey noise distortion.

"We normally wouldn't have noticed such a low frequency blast, but for some reason, it's being broadcast at very high power. The multi-frequency scanner caught it immediately."

"What is it?" the captain asked.

"That's where things start to get extra weird. It's Morse code. The old-fashioned kind. This was sent from an antique telegraph sounder."

"You're joking?"

"Not part of my job description, sir," she grinned.

"Where's it coming from?" he asked.

"The acoustic decay and sonar sequencing put it at one mile from our position."

"Heading?"

"Zero six zero," she replied.

"Anything on satellite or radar?"

"There wouldn't be."

The captain raised his eyebrows.

"Its location is pegged at 25,200 feet below us. That's just shy of five miles."

Captain Morris gave her his infamous WTF look that he used when he felt a crew member was trying to blow smoke where smoke shouldn't be blown.

"I've triple checked. One mile out, five miles down," Genna advised.

The captain listened to the beeping.

"It's an SOS."

Genna nodded.

Morris and Genna stared at each other.

He returned his com unit to auto.

"Brian – put us on a heading of zero six zero for one mile."

"Sir." Brian confirmed the orders.

Morris looked back down at Genna.

"*Sad Eyes*, I'm gonna need you guys to follow the coordinates that Genna's sending you now. We're receiving an SOS from about a mile from your current position."

"Roger that. Um – this may be a dumb question, Captain, but aren't you guys better equipped to reach the transmitting vessel than we are way down here?" Kendall asked.

"The SOS is coming from your depth. I repeat – the emergency signal is coming from down there with you. We show a range of 1,500 feet. Heading from your position is two eight zero," Morris advised.

"Roger that."

"I've patched the transmission through to *Sad Eyes*," Genna announced.

Craig entered a few key strokes to the com computer and the tiny vessel was suddenly filled with the sound of the faint beeps.

Kendall righted the sub to level flight position and killed the full brights and the video recorder. She nudged the throttle and put the submersible on the correct heading.

"You seeing anything on sonar?" she asked.

"Nothing that shouldn't be here," Craig replied.

"What exactly could transmit an SOS from this depth?"

"Nothing that I can think of. Besides, it's not just the depth. Who the hell would be using an old telegraph sounder?"

After ten minutes Kendall noticed that the seabed was rising ahead of the sub.

"*CO2*, the floor seems to have an incline that we don't have charted," Kendall said.

"Gradient?" Morris asked back.

"It's getting a little steep. I'm showing thirty-eight degrees and it's still rising."

The beeping suddenly stopped. The hiss and ambient distortion remained for a few seconds then everything went quiet.

"*CO2*, we have lost the SOS signal," Craig advised.

"Roger that," Genna replied. "It's gone up here too."

"This mound is getting steeper. I show forty-nine degrees now."

The regular external lights were enough to see the ocean floor beneath them but not much else. The laser sensors gave them a constant perimeter feed for up to fifty feet out.

"We're levelling," Kendall announced and she lowered the nose to keep parallel with the sea floor.

Suddenly the floor fell away sharply. Kendall slowed the craft immediately then lowered the nose to see where the bottom was taking them.

"Jesus," Craig cried. "Sonar contact ahead. Dead ahead – less than a hundred feet. Scrap that. It's everywhere. Oh my god. It's massive."

Kendall stopped the electric motors and brought *Sad Eyes* to a complete stop.

"You copying this up top?" Craig asked.

"We hear you," Morris replied. "What do you have down there?"

"No idea, but whatever it is – it's huge."

"How far ahead of you?"

"Sir, it's not ahead of us," Craig announced. "It's all around us."

"Going to full brights with recorders," Kendall announced.

The sad eyes exploded with light as their double beams cut through the blackness.

"Mother of God," Kendall whispered.

They were staring straight at the decayed superstructure of what had clearly been a very large ocean liner. They could clearly make out the bridge. Kendall suddenly saw movement two decks below. She had a momentary vision of what almost looked like people waving at her from where once had stood floor to ceiling windows.

The illusion lasted less than a second. By the time Kendall had blinked, all she could see was plankton and other tiny sea creatures illuminated by the harsh LED lights.

Craig moved up closer to his wife to have a better view.

"What the hell have we found?" he asked.

Kendall didn't answer.

"What's up?"

She muted her com device. "I thought I saw something. I thought I saw people waving at us?"

Craig patted her leg. "I'd have to say that nobody has waved from that ship for one hell of a long time."

"*Sad Eyes*, can I please get a sitrep?" Morris's voice boomed.

"We are hovering above what was undoubtedly the foredeck of a very large commercial vessel," Craig advised.

Kendall unmuted her com.

"I'm taking us forward to try and see if there's a name visible."

"There should be something on the bow just below the gunwale," Morris suggested.

"The ship is buried pretty deeply in the seabed. It looks like it hit the bottom hard. That mound we climbed seems to have been ocean-floor displacement when the ship reached the bottom," Kendall advised.

She guided the submersible over the bow and began descending alongside the hull. The entire ship was covered in marine life. The metal beneath had obviously been rusting for decades. Reddish green rusticles ran down the sides of the ship.

She stopped the descent when she saw something on the hull. Craig was watching from his camera array controller. He had the luxury of being able to zoom in on anything interesting.

"You seeing this?" Kendall asked.

"Looks like an S," Craig replied.

Kendall moved the sub slightly forward but couldn't make out any other letters.

"Can you move any closer?" Craig asked.

Kendall brought the sub to within a foot of the hull.

Craig took hold of the stick control for the port arm and gently guided it towards the ship. He tapped the grabber against its hull, just to the left of the S.

A large chunk of rusticles that had curled down from the gunwale, suddenly fell away.

"Oh my god!" Kendall's hand shot to her mouth.

"What's going on down there?" Morris asked.

"We have a name, sir." Kendall tried to keep the emotion from her voice. "You're not going to believe this but it's the *OCEANIS*."

There was dead silence from the com.

"Captain?" she tried again.

Kendall looked back at her husband. He just shrugged.

"Roger that," Captain Morris finally acknowledged. "You'd better start your ascent. The weather's closing in. Do you think you'll be able to locate her again?"

"To be perfectly honest, sir—" Kendall had trouble finding the right words. "We didn't locate her this time. She sent for us."

CHAPTER
TWENTY-FOUR

The crew of the *Columbus II* provided all their video footage and audio recordings the moment they notified NOAA headquarters in Maryland.

What no one, except a few members of the ship's crew, ever knew was that the notifying of NOAA had been delayed by almost an hour after *Sad Eyes* had been retrieved from the surface and its video had been evaluated.

Because of the extreme depth of operation, the sub operated without an umbilical. Video could not be fed back wirelessly to the surface. It was simply too much data to transmit in real time through five miles of water.

As soon as the submersible had been hoisted on board her umbilical was reattached. All the recorded video collected was immediately downloaded to the com mainframe.

Captain Morris had, as was protocol, wanted to satellite the video immediately to NOAA. Kendall took him aside and persuaded him to review one section of the recording before sharing it beyond their ship.

He was reluctant but she finally convinced him that he would never forgive himself if he didn't take a few minutes to view the footage.

They barged into COC. Morris was about to ask Genna to give them some privacy, but Kendall felt that she should see it as well.

Genna found the file and opened it up on her big screen. Kendall gave her an approximate time code which she found, then let the video play in real time.

It started a few seconds after the full brights were switched on showing the *Oceanis*'s superstructure.

"Focus on the deck two down from the bridge, roughly amidships," Kendall instructed.

They all saw the strange illusion of there being people waving but the vision only lasted a millisecond then the couple vanished among the sea life.

"Genna, please go back to the same place and slow it down to one frame a second."

Genna entered the data into the computer and replayed the moment. The superstructure was illuminated by the garish LED light. All eyes focused on the glassless window ports. The first frame showed a man and a woman with their hands raised in a wave. The next frame showed the same, but they weren't as clear, by the next frame they had partially dissolved. From then on the video showed nothing but water and sea life.

They watched the clip over twenty times.

"What do you think we are seeing?" Morris asked.

"It appears to be a man and a woman," Kendall replied.

"Which of course, it can't possibly be," Morris insisted. "So, I have to ask again – what exactly are we looking at?"

Genna pulled up the single isolated frame that showed the couple in the best resolution. She zoomed in to the man's face, then the woman's.

They all stared intently at the images.

"Those are people," Kendall stated.

"People do not live five miles beneath the surface of the ocean on sixty-year-old sunken wrecks," Morris argued. "It's a trick of light or something. It's like a Jesus image on a piece of toast. We're seeing them because our brains are wired to see human faces. The fact that they only appear for a fraction of a second proves that."

Genna continued zooming into different parts of the frozen image. She stopped on the left wrist of the man.

"I don't think our brains are wired to see wristwatches, are they?" Genna asked.

They looked as Genna increased the magnification. Thanks to the definition of the 4K camera, she was able to zoom in so much that the watch filled the screen.

"Omega," Kendall commented. "Nice watch."

The three continued to study the image but there was no doubt any more that they were looking at a watch, strapped to a man's wrist.

"You know, we are forgetting one other factor here," Genna mentioned.

"What?" Morris asked almost reluctantly.

"The Morse code transmission. We all heard it. We know it came from somewhere around that ship," Genna reminded them. "Who was sending it?"

"Oh, for God's sake. What are we saying? Ghosts sent us a message so we could find the ship? Why now? It's been over sixty-two years!"

"Not ghosts as such," Gemma spoke in almost a whisper. "But maybe some part of their life force remained on that ship. Almost 3,000 people died that day. How could there not be some psychic residue left behind?"

"Please don't come up with one of your metaphysical theories," Morris pleaded. "Have I got to remind you again that this is a scientific research ship. We don't do psychic."

Genna turned and gave him an almost pitying look. "If you only look for the scientific answer to everything, you miss out on some of the really good stuff. You asked why now? This area was hit with a massive earthquake just a few days ago. Doesn't that seem like a strange coincidence?"

"What are you suggesting? That the earthquake literally woke the dead?" Morris tried to sound incredulous but something about Genna's theory was starting to plug too many holes in the mystery to not be given some consideration.

"Genna, can you pull up the video from the first sensor recovery. I think it was number forty-seven."

Genna found the folder and after clicking on it, they saw that there were a number of videos to choose from.

"I'd like to see the initial discovery video, when *Sad Eyes* first located it."

"It's not very exciting," Kendall advised. "Just a whole lot of seabed footage."

"That's what I'm hoping for," he advised.

Genna played the first video from the list. It showed a barren ocean floor with almost no distinguishable variation to the flat, untouched surface.

"This is just about where we found it," Kendall said.

Sure enough, the quarter-ton yellow and red striped hexagonal device appeared at the bottom left corner of the image. The camera focused on the sensor as the sub was guided towards it.

The image suddenly flared with light.

"We put on the brights as we got closer."

The device was now mid frame and clearly illuminated.

"Freeze it there," Morris ordered.

Genna froze the frame. The damage to one side of the sensor was clearly visible.

"Zoom in on the seabed beyond the sensor."

Kendall looked over at him. "What are we looking for?"

"Something that shouldn't be there," he answered flatly.

Genna scanned the magnified image, section by section, from left to right.

She stopped on a dark discoloration on the sandy ocean floor.

"What is that?" Morris asked.

"I think it's a shadow," Kendall announced.

"Can you zoom in closer?" Morris requested.

"Absolutely," Genna said as she pulled in tighter to the anomaly. "It does look like a shadow."

"From what?" He approached the screen.

Genna continued to increase the magnification factor until they could see a piece of curved brass protruding from the sandy bottom.

"Holy shit!" Morris exclaimed.

"Is that what I think it is?" Genna asked.

"That's a very large piece of a very large propeller," Morris said. "It must have come from an incredibly big ship."

"Something like the size of the *Oceanis*?" Genna asked knowingly.

"Exactly like the size of the *Oceanis*," he replied.

"Is that what hit the sensor?" Kendall asked.

"It has to be. There wasn't anything else around it."

"How did it get a mile away from the wreck?" Kendall said.

"It must have come off the ship when it sank," Morris declared.

"And fell onto the sensor sixty-two years later?" Genna asked. "How much do you think that thing weighs?"

"Too much to have drifted a mile from the wreck," he stated.

The three glanced at each other wondering who was going to be the first to break the silence.

"They had to get our attention somehow," Genna said with a growing smile.

The three decided to commit an almost unheard-of breach of protocol. They vowed to never discuss what they had seen that day and what Genna had postulated. But their biggest concern was the frozen image of the couple. They did not want that picture to become the only thing remembered about the *Oceanis*. All lives had been lost when she sank without a trace. It was the worst maritime disaster of all time. They didn't feel that her history should be denigrated to nothing more than a creepy still image splashed across tabloids and even worse, being almost certainly turned into a viral meme of some sort. They made the decision to edit out the first frames of the video, then forwarded it to NOAA who then circulated it around the world.

Captain Morris, Kendall Davis and Genna Washington never spoke of what they'd seen again, however before deleting the frames, Genna printed one hard copy of the first frame for herself.

She didn't see the ghostliness or the sadness in those frames. She saw a couple in love who, for one last second, had been filled with hope.

CHAPTER
TWENTY-FIVE

Locating the *Oceanis* after over sixty years became the biggest news story on the planet. The ocean liner had gone missing in 1962. There had been no survivors and no idea of what had happened to the great ship. Her location became one of the greatest maritime mysteries of all time.

NOAA teams studied the fissures that surrounded the *Oceanis* and found a gigantic crumple zone on the sea floor some eighty miles from her final resting place. That plus extensive examination of the wreck itself finally led to the potential solving of the sixty-year-old mystery.

It was postulated that on the morning of 15 May 1962, there had been a severe subduction event between the Eurasian and North American tectonic plates. This caused a portion of the seabed to fracture. The eastern side of the fissure rose by over ten feet in a matter of seconds.

Having evaluated the remaining fissure and surrounding crumple zone, Caltech tectonic experts estimated that the earthquake could have measured as high as 9.3 on the Richter scale.

This would most certainly have resulted in a monster tsunami forming almost immediately. The high side of the seabed fracture would have forced trillions of gallons of water upwards.

Estimates based on computer simulations showed a wave of between 150 and 250 feet tall.

The simulations of the impact and subsequent sinking were based on the overall damage and structural conditions visible on the wreck.

It appeared that the ship had been steering into the wave when impact was made. Because of the stern having suffered the most dramatic damage, the simulation showed the *Oceanis* attempting to climb the wave wall. Within moments the vessel's own weight would have pulled it off the wave face, plunging it stern-first down into the ocean. It was believed that funnel number two separated from the ship at that point.

As the wave drew water into itself to sustain its size, the *Oceanis* was again drawn partially up the wall but was then pitch-poled back onto her stern only to have the base of the wave immediately lift her up again, in effect burying the bow, prow-first, under the water. She never resurfaced again.

She had travelled to the bottom at an estimated forty-five miles an hour. She struck the seabed at approximately a thirty-degree angle causing the hull to bury itself in the ocean floor.

The force of the impact caused a seabed crater mound that surrounded the ship to a height of almost a hundred feet. In effect, it had created its own sonar barrier at the bottom of the ocean.

The barrier made it almost impossible for the wreck to have ever been found.

EPILOGUE

Three months after the *Oceanis* had been located, a memorial service was held at St Patrick's Cathedral in New York. It was streamed live around the world. Family members of the passengers and crew gathered across the globe to finally say their goodbyes to those that had vanished sixty years earlier.

Many people spoke at the service. The most anticipated was Maureen Hess, the wife of the ship's first officer. She had married the dashing Commander Isaac Hess only two years before losing him. She was last to speak and was by far the eldest person to address the congregation that day.

She was in her late eighties, frail and a bit startled by all the recent attention. She was helped to the pulpit by her two sons as her six grandchildren looked on.

She gazed out over the crowded cathedral then donned a pair of heavy-rimmed glasses. She read from her own notes.

"Sixty-two years ago, I waved goodbye to my husband for an absence that should have been no longer than a fortnight. I stood on the dock in Southampton and looked up at the bridge wing where I knew he would be. That was our little tradition before each voyage. I would always wear as silly a hat as I could find so he would see me among the dockside crowd. I would wave until he spotted me, at which point he would blow me a kiss. That shared gesture was somehow sufficient to carry me through his usual fortnight absence at sea.

"On that occasion, I was pregnant with our second child and I never thought for a second that that blown kiss would have to last me for a lifetime. I never saw him again and worse, up until today, never knew what had befallen him and everyone else on board the *Oceanis*.

"Over the years we all heard the theories. Some were honest attempts at solving the mystery. Some were outright conspiracies about sabotage or her being sunk intentionally by the crew. But mostly what we heard were the ramblings of the mentally unhinged, hoping for their fifteen minutes of vulgar fame. There were reports of the ship being seen in South America where the passengers and crew had set up their own commune. There were those who swore they had seen her afloat within the Bermuda Triangle or stranded in the frozen waters of Antarctica. There were even those who believed that alien beings had taken the entire vessel off the planet for study.

"The one thing I never heard was that anyone had actually found the ship. Imagine my surprise when I turned on the nightly news three months ago and saw her lying on the bottom of the Atlantic. Alone and neglected. A little like myself on some days.

"2,722 lives were lost on that day, yet no one knew what had happened. The *Oceanis* must have undergone extraordinary destructive forces on that tragic morning, yet no one knew.

"The souls of all of those on board had been waiting over sixty years to pass onto the next plane. But they couldn't make the ultimate transition without their loved ones knowing of their entombment at the bottom of the Atlantic Ocean.

"Three months ago, they were found. Their mortal bodies had long gone, but their spirits had remained waiting for all this time for the rusted hulk of the *Oceanis* to be found so they could finally move on.

"At long last the souls of 2,722 people were released from the confinement of the ravaged ship and permitted to rise up, knowing that all of us are now aware of their fate and are at last able to say our goodbyes."

Maureen Hess took a breath and looked up to the heavens.

"My dearest Tony. It's been a very long time. You should know that I did wait for you. You were in my heart and in my mind for every second of those sixty-two years. I have little doubt that I will be with you soon, my love. Please try and wait for me."

She lowered her head and quietly shed a few tears as her family, the congregation and the world looked on.

A thousand miles away and five miles beneath the surface of the Atlantic, the rusted hulk of the *SS Oceanis* sat in silence in a world of complete darkness.

There were no submersibles diving on her that day.

She was entirely on her own.

There was no one to witness the brief flash of blue light that ran from bow to stern within the wreckage, as the ravaged shell of the once majestic liner gave off one last glimmer of life before giving way to the elements that would ultimately reduce her to nothing more than a temporary discoloration on the ocean floor.